The Island of Misfit Boys

The Island of Misfit Boys

A Xenofreak Nation Novel

By Melissa Conway

This is a work of fiction. Names, characters, businesses, organizations, places, events and incidents are the product of the author's imagination or are used fictitiously. Any resemblance to actual persons, living or dead, is coincidental.

Chapter One

New York, April 2034

"I'm Ellie. You're Freya. Last name Jones."

"Freya" yanked the top drawer out of her dresser and dumped its contents next to the bulging black garbage bag on the futon that served as her bed.

"Jones?" she asked with an upward quirk of one eyebrow.

Her mother shrugged. "Mags didn't have time to research names you might find suitable."

"Freya's fine, I guess. Better than Chrissie."

Chrissie had been, until moments ago, Freya's name. It had replaced her birth name, Amanda, more than three months ago, when she and her mother had first gone on the run.

"Hey," Ellie said. "Take some of that out of there. Only what you can carry. And hurry up."

Freya dug through the plastic bag. Under her karate gi, she found and removed a couple of heavy sweaters she wouldn't need now that the weather was warmer. "Where are we going?"

"Brooklyn."

"What?" The worst of the rioting had occurred there.

"Ryan found us a place. We'll be staying with a woman he says can be trusted."

"Wouldn't it be safer to leave New York?"

"Ryan and Mags can't help us outside of the five boroughs."

Freya sighed, but didn't argue.

In the hallway, they passed Mrs. Aguilar, who didn't fail to notice Freya and Ellie were bogged down with bags. "I'd offer to help," she said, "but, you know, my sciatica. You got clothes in those bags? Because if you're donating them, my sister's girls could use them."

"No, this is just poor-man's luggage," Ellie said with a smile.

"Oh, you going on a trip?" Mrs. A. had always been a bit nosy.

"Just a few days. Family visit."

"Okay, don't worry, I'll keep an eye on your apartment for you."

"Thanks. See you soon."

Or never, Freya thought, but she didn't feel so much as a pang of regret at leaving this place. Eventually, the skeevy landlord would figure out they'd gone, and she only wished she could see his face when he realized they'd skipped out on the rent. No doubt he'd confiscate and sell the belongings they'd left behind, but what little they had was second-hand anyway.

A black sedan idled at the curb in front of the building. The driver, her cousin Ryan, popped the trunk and got out to help them. He rearranged the items in the trunk, moving aside a bullhorn, a pair of huge bolt cutters and what Freya thought might be a shotgun, before stuffing their belongings in and slamming the lid.

On the road, her mother tilted her 'traveling hat' so her face was partially hidden behind its wide rim. It was one of numerous strategies she and Freya had adopted to avoid the city's many cameras, and the possibility that their enemies might find them through facial recognition software. The windows in the back of the sedan were privacy tinted, but Freya sank down in the seat just in case.

"How's the leg?" Ellie asked.

Freya saw Ryan's shoulder move, and assumed he was rubbing his thigh, where he'd taken a bullet right before her life had changed drastically for the worse.

"All healed," he said. "Graduated physical therapy with flying colors."

He put his hand back on the steering wheel, and Freya studied his knuckles. There were no scars where his xenograft used to be. Ryan Boardman was an XIA agent who'd been held in quarantine after the riots because he'd been exposed to the supertyphoid that had swept the city and killed so many non-xenos. His particular grafts, from the skin of an alligator bioengineered to be compatible with humans, would have turned him into a carrier of the disease. It had taken several weeks after the grafts had been removed for the CDC to determine he was no longer a danger to the public and he'd been released.

Of their many relatives, he was the only one who completely understood the gravity of their situation, and how essential discretion was. Everyone else knew they were in hiding but had no idea where they were or why they'd gone underground.

"You're sure you were recognized?" he asked.

"Pretty sure," Freya said.

Ryan looked at her in the rearview mirror. "Tell me."

Freya took a breath and launched into the story. "On Monday at school, fourth quarter started, and I had to take Health class. This guy I'd seen around but never talked to sat at the desk next to me. Right off the bat he's staring at me, like, all period long. You know, kinda creepy? Then the next day I notice him everywhere, like he's following me around."

"What's his name?"

"Trevor Segal."

"He talk to you?"

"Yeah. Today he stops me in the quad and says, 'Do I know you?'"

"What'd you say?"

"I'm like, no, dude, never seen you before. Then he grabs my arm and puts his mouth right next to my ear and goes, 'I don't know what you're doing, but you better knock it the hell off.'"

"Language," her mom said.

"Well, that's what he said," Freya replied. "And he really scared me. Like worse than anything."

"Is that it?" Ryan asked.

"Isn't that enough?" Freya was suddenly on the defensive. Did Ryan think she'd overreacted?

Ellie gave him a stern look. "He asked if he knew her, Ryan."

"Yeah, I know. Definitely a red flag. What did he think you were doing, though?"

"No idea," Freya said.

"Could he have been involved with the killers?" Ellie asked.

"If he was, I doubt he would have confronted her."

"How do you know?" Ellie said. "Maybe whoever did this hates xenos."

Ryan sighed. "My working theory doesn't involve a hate crime."

Hate *crime?* Freya thought. *Try "crimes."*

There'd been seventeen deaths over the course of two weeks, six in a lab explosion and the rest in various "accidents." All the dead had been associated, either as staff or patients, with a company called Falconot Biomedical. Freya and her mother had gotten to know most of the deceased during the two years Freya participated in a small clinical research trial run by the company. Everything had begun to fall apart soon after someone hacked the National Library of Medicine and released the study to the public, along with dozens of other studies involving bioengineered animal skin grafts.

3

She looked out the window, noticing Ryan had taken the wrong road. "I thought we were going to Brooklyn."

"Just taking precautions in case we have a tail. Been having to do that a lot lately."

"You've been followed?" Ellie asked.

"More than once. Tried to ID the vehicles but came up empty. Of course, it might not have anything to do with you. Got a lot on my plate."

"Well, we really appreciate everything you've done."

"I wish I could help in an official capacity."

Her mother produced a scoffing sound but didn't reply.

"If it's any consolation," Ryan said, "my supervisor thinks we should open an investigation. Unfortunately, she can't convince the director because the Singh lawsuit is burying us and the director's just trying to keep the agency afloat."

"Is your job at risk?" Ellie asked.

"I was one of the last agents hired, so I'll be first to go if it comes to it. Plus, I helped blow up Singh's yacht, so…yeah."

"I'm sorry. I hope we aren't jeopardizing–"

"You're not."

Freya closed her eyes, half-listening to the rest of the conversation. She hated having to move again. Hated starting over with another new name. But most of all, she hated that the fear was back. It had taken weeks for her to settle into their new reality, and longer to come to terms with the fact that she was the reason they were hiding.

After an hour or so, Ryan pulled into an apartment complex and parked in spot 320. They all got out, and he took both garbage bags full of clothes out of his trunk and carried them into the building. Freya brought up the rear as they ascended two flights of stairs to the third floor. Ryan knocked on a door halfway down the hallway and it immediately opened.

The woman who answered was middle-aged and shorter than Freya by a few inches. She had thin, light brown hair with blonde streaks. Over her shoulder, Freya saw that the small apartment was tidy. It smelled of pine-scented floor cleaner that almost masked the odor of cigarette smoke.

"Come on in. I'm Carla, but people call me Mouse." She glanced at the bags. "Is that all there is?"

Ryan nodded and set the bags down next to the couch.

Mouse made a little *tsk* sound, but then smiled impishly. "Believe it or not, you aren't the first house guests I've had who've been on the run."

Freya smiled back and relaxed ever-so-slightly. Just as she was thinking maybe this wouldn't be as bad as she'd expected, Mouse held up a box of hair color in one hand and some scissors in the other.

"Who's first?"

Chapter Two

Dan Corvi ducked under the caution tape stretched across the doorframe of the abandoned house and followed his friend Bass inside. Late afternoon sunlight slanted in through busted-out windows. The walls that were still intact were blackened from the fire that had gutted the place, and the ones that weren't intact were destroyed in such a way that it was obvious someone had already scavenged the wiring and pipes.

"Nothing left," he said.

Bass winked and waved him in further.

Dan directed a skeptical look at the wooden floor, which creaked with every step, but he cautiously made his way to what had once been the kitchen. Bass stopped a few feet short of the entranceway because the floor inside the kitchen had collapsed into the crawl space. The sagging cabinets along the back wall looked like they were hanging by a thread, their open doors revealing the emptiness inside.

"See there?" Bass pointed to the scorched copper backsplash.

"Not worth dying for." Dan started back, but Bass tossed out a challenging, "You scared?"

"No. Just not stupid."

"Well, I'm going for it." Bass took one step, and the house protested with an ominous groaning sound. He froze. "Or not."

"Come on, let's get out of here. This place is a death trap." Dan moved quickly to the front door, stepping over the threshold and walking right though the caution tape, relieved to obtain the relative safety of the concrete porch.

Bass wasn't so lucky. When he was halfway across the main room, the floor gave way. The edge adjacent to the kitchen dropped out from under him, tearing floorboards loose or snapping them like tinder. Dan caught a glimpse of his friend's shocked face right before a cloud of moldy-smelling dust filled the room and rolled out the front door.

"Bass!" he shouted, waving a hand to clear the dust. "You okay?"

He heard coughing, and then a weak, "Yeah, I think so."

"I'll get help!"

"No!" Bass said. "My dad'll kill me. I'm not hurt. Just help me get out of here."

As the dust began to dissipate and Dan got a good look at the damage, he debated whether to call for help anyway, but decided against it. Bass's father wouldn't so much care that his son had gotten himself into this situation as much as he would care about the cost of getting him out of it. Since none of this would have happened if Bass hadn't been trespassing, the city would surely bill his father for emergency services, and their family was just as bad off as Dan's.

Kneeling on the porch, Dan couldn't do anything to help other than give suggestions on foot and hand holds as his friend climbed slowly and carefully towards him. It seemed to take forever but was probably closer to ten minutes by the time Dan grabbed his hand and hoisted him to safety.

The two young men lay on their backs looking up at the sky and laughed. After they caught their breath, they decided to beat a hasty retreat before anyone in the neighborhood investigated. As they walked towards the block where they both lived, Dan gestured to Bass's head. "You got something in your hair."

Bass bent at the waist and ran his fingers through his thick red hair to dislodge the dirt. "You're not exactly spotless yourself."

Dan brushed his hands down the front of his filthy shirt with little effect. The inside of his nose itched, and his eyes felt like they had grit in them. It occurred to him that breathing the dust from the old house couldn't have been healthy – but then again, life in Brooklyn these days wasn't healthy in general.

In the parking lot of their apartment complex, Bass split off for his building. "Later."

Dan nodded and entered the building closest to the street. He took the steps two at a time to the third floor, wanting to get a quick shower before his mom got home and saw him. His dad was sitting on the couch watching holovision.

"Hey Dad."

Randolph Corvi looked up and smiled vaguely at his son. Four months ago, he would have given Dan major flak for coming home looking like he'd been buried alive, but that was before the riots. Now, still recovering from the traumatic brain injury he'd sustained attempting to protect the family business from rioters, he didn't seem to notice Dan's appearance.

7

Dan ducked into the bathroom and stripped off his clothes, stuffing them into the hamper. He cranked the faucet to hot and glanced in the mirror while the water warmed up. He didn't look quite as bad as Bass, but the dust had given his olive-toned skin a ghostly bent.

When he got out of the shower, he wrapped a towel around his hips and opened the door. His mother stood there with a surprised look on her face, fist raised like she'd been about to knock.

"Oh!" she said. "What are you doing?"

"What's it look like?" Dan angled his upper body away, hoping she wouldn't notice the reddish-brown scales wrapped around his upper arm.

She grinned and poked him in the stomach with her finger. "Look at those abs."

Dan felt his cheeks go hot. "Mom."

She sighed and reached up to brush his wet hair back. He suffered through her ministrations, but only because she'd been so sad lately.

"You plan on growing it all the way to your shoulders?" Her question was a passive aggressive protest that only made him want to grow his hair longer, even though he had to use a ton of product to tame his dark brown curls as it was.

Suddenly, she exclaimed, "Is that a *xenograft*?" Her expression and tone conveyed shocked outrage.

He tried to slip past her, mumbling, "It's no big deal, Mom."

She grabbed his left arm to stop him, and even though he was incredibly uncomfortable standing there in nothing but a towel, he didn't pull away.

"Explain," she said in an ice-cold voice. "This minute."

He'd hoped to hide it from her indefinitely, but now that the secret was out, he launched into the persuasive speech he'd prepared. "I'm eighteen now, and the graft didn't cost anything. Plus, it'll protect me in case the supertyphoid–"

"What do you mean it didn't cost anything?" she barked.

"I got it for free, and they're actually paying me."

Her face scrunched up in exaggerated confusion. "Someone *paid* you to get a xenograft."

"Pays. Every week I fill out an online survey, and they deposit twenty bucks into my savings account."

"Who?"

"It's for research. Come on, Mom. Lemme get dressed."

She stared into his eyes for a moment longer, so he'd know the conversation wasn't over, and then moved aside.

He went into his room and closed the door before heaving a sigh of relief.

Chapter Three

"Freya. I'm Freya Jones," she said to herself in the mirror mounted near the front door of Mouse's apartment. The girl who stared back had hair that was a couple of shades lighter than her natural dark blonde, and a fresh new haircut that was much shorter than she was used to having, a pixie cut that she had to admit didn't look half bad. The bangs slanting jaggedly above her blue eyes gave her a toughness she didn't feel, but sorely needed.

She slung her borrowed backpack over one shoulder and consulted the note in her hand. Temple Grandin High School was six blocks away. According to Ryan, there were four cameras to watch out for between the school and the apartment complex; one traffic cam, and three security cams. The best route in order to avoid them all was to go four blocks east and then two blocks south.

She'd been surprised that her mother insisted she finish high school. It seemed like a completely avoidable risk to Freya, but her mother had said, "Your father would turn over in his grave if you didn't go to college."

Freya's argument that a diploma under a fake name wouldn't be valid anyway was rejected out of hand.

"You're going to stay in school, and that's final," her mom had said. "Whoever's after us won't expect it, so it's probably the safest place for you. Besides, Mags already registered you."

Maggie "Mags" Finlay had been Ellie's best friend since grade school. She was an administrator in the New York City Department of Education, with access to add and delete school records in the statewide system, which is how Freya had obtained her shiny new identity and stellar grades.

Too stellar, she thought as she took the stairs to the lobby and then walked out into the overcast morning. Freya had always been a good student, but Mags had given her a 4.0 average, something she doubted she could live up to. Not that it mattered. Before her father had gotten sick, there'd been money set aside for Freya's future, but that was gone. Her mother was a veterinarian, but she couldn't work in that trade anymore without risking discovery. Mouse had gotten her a job at a place called Bluto's, a dive bar out on what was left of Coney Island, whose manager wasn't concerned that Ellie didn't have ID. The under-the-counter pay was dismal, and the tips scanty. There wouldn't be enough money for Freya to attend even the cheapest of community colleges.

She walked fast, but after three blocks slowed down because she'd caught up with a couple of boys walking ahead of her and didn't want to pass them. Something about the boys, especially the taller of the two, made her eye them warily. They were dressed innocuously enough in jeans and hoodies, but she felt it best to avoid them. At the next corner, she crossed the street, forgetting about them until she arrived in front of her new high school. As she stood staring in dismay at the ancient and unkempt one-story building, she saw the boys join up with a larger group loitering nearby.

Averting her gaze so she wouldn't make eye contact with any of them, she strode through the open front doors, passing through an automated weapons detector. Several steps in, as the noise of the crowded hallway assaulted her, her bravado faltered. Mouse had tried to prepare her for the reality of her new existence.

"Temple Grandin was a nice school until the riots, when it burned to the ground. They reopened it in a new location, but that's the only thing new about it. The building was an elementary school fifty years ago, then it was a vocational training center, and now it's a high school. From what I understand, it's kind of a rough place."

"Is she going to be in danger there?" her mother had asked.

Mouse shrugged. "She's a xeno, so that'll give her some protection. We tend to stick together."

"She can't tell anyone about her graft, though."

"Why not?"

Her mother wrinkled her nose. "It's not your average graft. If word gets out what she's got, then she'll *definitely* be in danger."

The bell rang before Freya managed to find the office. Once she did, the school secretary pulled up her information on a holoscreen, and then asked if Freya had a digital copy of her certificate of health.

Freya blinked in confusion as her anxiety skyrocketed. Not long after the riots, the state of New York, in an effort to prevent any more xeno-related epidemics, had instituted a requirement that all registered students, from elementary school on up, be examined by a physician to determine whether they had a xenograft, and what kind it was. Prior to the supertyphoid outbreak, it was not only considered unusual for a child to

11

have one, but borderline abusive. That had changed as word got out that grafts purportedly protected the host against the infection, and frightened parents everywhere had rushed their children to xenograft dens.

Mags told Freya's mother that they couldn't fake a health certificate because the digital documents were encoded with a signature of authenticity, but that she could indicate in Freya's file that the certificate had been verified. That had worked at her last school, but apparently not here.

"Um, I—I don't have a holophone," she said, which wasn't true, but the phone Ryan had given her was a burner strictly for emergencies.

Freya was on the verge of offering to run "home" for it, when the secretary said, "Oh, wait. Never mind. It's been verified. I'll print you a class schedule."

Freya let out a little sigh of relief as the secretary told her where to find her first class.

Mags had signed Freya up for all advanced placement classes. Freya suspected she'd done it in order to minimize her exposure to the school's more undesirable students, not that there was any guarantee that smart kids couldn't also be scary. The end result was that after her first four classes, she found herself in way over her head academically.

Lunch hour was an eye-opening experience. She entered the cafeteria and looked around for a suitable table, spotting a good candidate near the garbage can that had four girls and one nerdy-looking guy, all of them staring at their holophones. She sat at the far end of the table, but before she could even open her paper lunch sack, one of the girls said, "Hey! New girl."

Freya looked up, keeping a neutral look on her face. From the challenging tone, she knew the girl wanted to start something, and it wasn't a conversation.

"Who said you could sit here?" the girl demanded. She wore heavy black eyeliner and outweighed Freya by at least thirty pounds.

Freya's heart began to beat faster, but she stared her down. "I did."

The girl placed her fists on the table and half-stood. "Oh, you think you're tough?"

Freya didn't break eye contact. "No, but I *can* defend myself."

One week after she and her mother had abandoned their home and left everything and everyone behind, they'd signed up for a free twice weekly self-defense class at the local community center. It had started out as a way to defuse some of the fear, but once Freya got her certification, she found she'd developed a need to take it to the next level. She'd volunteered to work in the office at the community center after school and had gotten a few months of intensive karate and kickboxing training for free in return. Her new skills had boosted her confidence to unprecedented levels.

Not that she enjoyed confrontation or intimidation, as this girl seemed to.

"Knock it off, Cindy," the boy at the table said. He was small and thin, with acne-pocked cheeks. He glanced at Freya. "She's harmless."

"No, I'm not," Cindy said belligerently.

"She gets aggressive when her blood sugar's low," one of the other girls said without looking up from her holophone.

"No, I don't." Cindy sat back down.

"She's just protective of us," another girl said.

"That's true," Cindy said. "Who else is gonna do it?"

Freya tentatively opened her paper sack and took out her sandwich, hoping that was the end of it.

The third girl spoke up. "What's your name?"

The boy answered for her. "It's Freya. She's in my calculus class."

"Well, you've met Cindy," said the third girl, who had long black hair and a round face. "I'm Jin, spelled J-I-N, as in genie. That's Sandrew–"

"A combination of my mom and dad's names," the boy said. "Because they *wanted* me to be a pariah."

"And that's Gev–"

"You're not gay, are you?" Gev asked. She had an upturned nose and a partially grown out mohawk with faint streaks of purple blended into her blonde hair.

Freya's mouth was full of bologna and cheese, so she just shook her head.

"Pity 'cause you're pretty," Gev said, quoting lyrics from a popular song.

"And that's Kaye," Jin finished, gesturing to a dark-skinned girl with black eyes and curly hair barely contained under several clips. "Got it? There'll be a quiz at the end of lunch period."

Gev moved to sit across from Freya. "Why'd you choose our table?"

"Because from here I can see the whole room."

Gev frowned. "Hm. Surprisin' answer. I thought you picked it because you figured we'd leave you alone."

Freya made a rueful face. "That, too."

Kaye scooted down the bench closer to Gev. "Well, you made an error in judgement."

"Uh-oh," Sandrew said. "Here comes the inquisition."

Kaye didn't miss a beat. "Where you from?"

Freya and her mother had worked out a fictitious history, but it was bare bones. If these kids were as tenacious as she suspected, it wouldn't hold up under their bombardment of questions. Still, she couldn't very well ignore them.

"San Diego." First lie.

"Military?" Gev asked.

"My dad was." Second lie.

Kaye leaned forward on her elbows. "Was?"

"He died a few years ago." That part was true. Her father had died from colorectal cancer, but if they asked, she would tell them it had been a car accident.

"Sorry," Kaye said. "You live with your mom?"

Freya took another bite and nodded.

"You joining any clubs?" Jin asked.

"Um...maybe."

"We're all members of Hologame Club. I'm Jin-san. Hyphenated."

She pointed to each of the others, who responded with their screen names. Gev said, "Blootenwart," Cindy said, "Viragosh," Kaye said, "Vampeth," and Sandrew said, "Einsteinfranken, but she probably doesn't even know what Hologame Club is."

"Everyone knows what Hologame Club is." Cindy raised her eyebrows at Freya, who nodded in the affirmative. Hologame Club had been the hottest social media site for the last two years in a row.

"We meet online every afternoon," Jin said. "Interested?"

"Look at her," Sandrew said. "She doesn't exactly scream Hologame player."

Jin shook her head at him scornfully. "Since when do *we* judge people based on their appearance?"

"Since they judge us."

Jin turned back to Freya. "Please excuse his bitterness. It's pretty much ingrained at this point."

"I'll bet you a million bucks she's never played a hologame in her life," Sandrew said.

Everyone looked at Freya, who responded, "True, but only because we couldn't afford it."

"Ha!" Jin crowed, grinning triumphantly at Sandrew. "Need I remind you what happens when you assume?"

"Maybe if we stopped bickering long enough to listen to her answer...?" Kaye suggested.

14

It took Freya a moment to recall the original question. She *wasn't* interested in Hologame Club, but felt it'd be more diplomatic not to admit it. "I've got a pretty full schedule."

"Figures," Sandrew muttered, looking back down at his holophone.

The disappointment at the table felt almost palpable. Freya scrambled to think of a bone she could toss their way. "You guys work out? I could use a sparring partner."

Everyone burst out laughing, even Cindy. "Do we look like we work out?"

Freya shrugged. "You asking me to judge?"

"Aaand she throws our words back into our faces," Sandrew said.

"That's because she's smart," Jin replied. "Which you would have noticed if you weren't so high up on that horse – or should I say donkey?"

He shot her a dirty look. "Thanks a not."

"You're schwelcome."

Freya finished her sandwich and sat there uncomfortably trying to think of an excuse to leave the cafeteria, but then the bell rang, saving her the trouble.

"Saved by the bell?" Jin asked.

Freya smiled. "I'm a bit overwhelmed. You know, new school."

Jin placed her palms on the table and leaned towards her. "It's really not that bad here, and you're welcome to hang with us any time."

"Thanks. I appreciate that."

Freya left for her next class, thinking if things had been different, she might actually *want* to hang with them.

Chapter Four

The new girl Dan had noticed on the way to school was in his P.E. class. She was tall and thin, but not awkwardly so. A lot of twiggy girls reminded him of those old 2D Popeye cartoons, he couldn't remember the female character's name, but she'd been skinny and graceless. Even wearing gym clothes a size too big, the new girl managed to look good.

Mr. Gillan sent the class out to the back field to run a warmup lap. "I don't want to see anyone walking today! Anyone walks, the rest of the class keeps running for the entire period!"

A groan rose up from some of the students, mostly the out-of-shape ones. Dan was tempted to hang back to make sure none of them stopped, but the new girl had already broken into a fast jog and he wanted to get a better look at her. He caught up and settled several paces behind her, admiring the rear view. When they went into the first turn, heading into the wind, the air of her slipstream passed over and around him, redolent with her aroma. It was a scent unlike anything he could recall smelling, and yet was strangely familiar. It wasn't perfume exactly, more like something he might want to eat, like sizzling bacon or steak on the grill. His mouth actually watered until he broke away from the pack and sprinted around her. In passing, he caught a glimpse of her bare neck, and had the highly disturbing urge to tackle her and take a bite out of it.

Normally an adequate but unenthusiastic runner, he was the first person across the finish line.

Mr. Gillan split the class into two groups, and further divided the groups into teams for basketball. The new girl went off with her team to the far court, and Dan found himself grateful she'd been removed from his vicinity.

After school, he saw her again as he walked home with Bass. She was on the other side of the street ahead of them, striding along rapidly, as if she couldn't wait to put distance between herself and the school.

"You got the new girl in any of your classes?" he asked.

Bass picked up a rock and lobbed it at a tree. "What new girl? She cute?"

"The blonde across the street."

Bass swiveled his head until he spotted her. "What's her name?"

"Uh, her gym shirt said Jones." All students were required to write their last names on their jerseys in permanent marker.

To Dan's irritation, Bass shouted, "Hey, Jones!"

Thankfully, she didn't seem to hear him. Dan thumped him on the shoulder. "Why you gotta do that?"

Bass grinned. "So she *is* cute. You like her?"

"Don't know her. She…smells good."

With a leer and a chuckle, Bass said, "Don't they all. Except Lisa Warren. I kinda had a crush on her until I got close enough to smell her perfume. Same as my mom's. Total turn-off."

The sound of a badly tuned engine alerted them just before Wade Limberg and company pulled up next to them. Wade was a friend of sorts – but Dan and Bass only hung out with him to stay off his radar. Privately, they joked that Wade would be voted "Most likely to get life in prison." His posse, Mick and Donnie, didn't even get that much respect; Dan doubted they would live long enough to get life.

From the driver's seat of the ancient Jeep Wrangler, Wade called, "Hey, Danny Boy. Bass."

Dan kept walking. "Sup, Wade."

"We're going to the park." Wade leaned past Mick in the passenger seat and showed them a paper bag that obviously held a bottle, probably something alcoholic, and definitely something cheap. "You wanna come along?"

"Nah, gotta take my dad to a doctor appointment."

"Next time." Wade drove off but didn't go far. He turned left and slowed down, keeping pace with the new girl as she walked.

Dan rolled his eyes at Wade's catcall, "I want me some of *that!*"

If Jones said anything in reply, Dan was too far away to hear it, but he knew Wade well enough to hope she kept her mouth shut.

He and Bass crossed the street. They were about half a block behind Jones when Wade put the jeep in park and got out. Jones stopped walking and faced him, arms crossed defensively. The sweat on Wade's shaved head glinted in the afternoon sun, the skull tattoo on his crown giving him a barbaric look.

"Uh, oh," Bass said. "Looks like Wade likes the way she smells, too."

"Shut up." Dan squinted in an attempt to read Jones' lips. Wade, loudmouth that he was, he could hear.

"Name's Wade. Me and my friends are going to the park. You wanna come?"

They were close enough now that Dan could pick out the words, "No, thank you."

She said it politely, but to Wade, any form of disagreement was a challenge.

"Think you're too good for me?"

"I don't know you."

"Well, that's why I invited you. So we could get to know each other."

Jones didn't respond; she just regarded Wade warily.

Predictably, his eyes narrowed menacingly. "Or you could just tell me you're not interested."

Before she could seal her fate by saying it, Dan walked up. "Hey Jones. How's it going?"

She looked up into Dan's face, no recognition in her eyes. "Fine."

He moved closer and bent his head, inhaling deeply. God, she smelled good. A completely unwelcome sense of possession overcame him and before he knew it, his hand had wrapped itself around her elbow.

"I'll walk you home," he murmured.

"Dude," Wade said. "Back off."

Dan didn't intend to confront Wade, but as if some perverse spirit had taken control of his mouth, he heard the words, "No, *you* back off," come out of it.

Wade sneered, but before he could respond, Jones yanked her arm out of Dan's grasp. "You're both crazy. Leave me alone!"

She stalked off, and Dan had to fight the impulse to chase after her. As the bizarrely intoxicating effect of her presence wore off, he said, "I have no idea why I did that."

"Like the girl said," Wade responded, "you're crazy."

Dan was already knee deep into it, so instead of backing down, he said, "She's a nice girl, Wade. Not your type."

"What, because I only like sluts?" Wade's outrage was badly feigned.

Logic wasn't normally a successful strategy with Wade, but Dan tried anyway. "You wanted her to go to the park with you to get drunk. She wasn't interested."

For a moment it seemed like Wade wasn't going to let it go, but then he laughed. "Yeah, well, she's obviously not interested in you, either."

Dan had no intention of reinforcing his claim on her, right up until the words, "We'll see," bubbled up and spouted forth.

Wade's face exhibited genuine surprise, and a hint of respect. "You really got it bad, don'cha Danny Boy? Bad enough to take me on?"

Dan rubbed his eyes, confused, embarrassed, and kind of scared at his own behavior. "Didn't mean to get in your face."

Wade was the least understanding person of Dan's acquaintance, but *this* he seemed to get. "Girls'll mess a guy up that way."

Bass, who'd been silently observing, chimed in. "Right?"

Wade shot him a dismissive glance and turned back to Dan. "You get a free pass...this time."

Dan and Bass stood on the sidewalk in a cloud of exhaust as the Wrangler sped off.

"What the hell just happened?" Bass asked.

"I have no freaking idea," Dan replied fervently.

Chapter Five

The next morning, Freya left the apartment ten minutes early specifically to avoid running into either of the young men she'd encountered the day before. Wade, the bald, tattooed guy, had been pushy and obnoxious, but the tall, dark-haired one who'd called her Jones had actually frightened her more. Something about the way he'd leaned towards her, invading her personal space in a manner much more intimate than Wade's blunt come-on, made her want to run and hide somewhere deep underground.

When she reached the school campus, she headed straight for the main entrance, but Cindy waylaid her.

"Freya. I wanted to say I'm sorry for yesterday."

"It's okay." Freya smiled and tried to continue on her way.

"You wanna hang with us?"

Freya looked around. Gev, Kaye, Sandrew and Jin were standing near the flagpole. Jin grinned and waved.

"I'd like that, but I really need to get a jump-start on today's Language Arts less–"

Cindy clapped her on the back with a beefy hand, forcing her to take a step towards the others. "Great!"

Guess that's settled, Freya thought, as Cindy escorted her over to her friends.

"Good morning, Freya," Jin said. "I love that name, by the way."

"Thanks. Likewise."

"You weren't about to, uh, go inside, were you?" Sandrew asked.

The way he said it sounded as if she'd been about to make a grave mistake.

"Yeah, why?"

Every one of them began shaking their heads.

"Tuesday is Spirit Day," Gev said.

Freya eyed them suspiciously. "And…?"

Kaye turned to Jin. "I don't know, she's pretty enough to be the cheerskank type."

"She wouldn't have sat at our table if she had the chops," Jin replied.

"Chops? *Chops?!*" Gev exclaimed.

"Sorry. Bad word choice. I meant…if she had the inclination."

"Well, she's clearly sane, so how could she possibly be so inclined?" Gev retorted.

"I don't know, but with her looks, the cheerskanks might try to recruit her." Kaye shrugged.

Freya had a feeling they would continue talking around and about her until first bell rang, so she attempted to interrupt. "I'm not–"

"It's way too late in the season," Sandrew said. "Nobody's recruiting anybody."

"Yeah, but they're one short. Terri Hackworth had to drop out." Jin nodded sagely, patting her stomach.

"Forgot about that."

Freya raised her voice. "You guys."

The five friends looked at her expectantly.

"I'm not interested in being a cheerleader. Why can't I go inside?"

All of them began talking at once. Freya looked from face to face as they spoke, barely managing to get the gist of it – that the cheerleaders were lying in wait for students in the main hallway in an attempt to drum up enthusiasm for Temple Grandin's lame sports teams.

Then a weird thing happened. The gentle morning breeze lifted the little hairs on the back of Freya's neck, sending chill bumps down her spine, but instead of subsiding after the breeze faded away, the sensation persisted. As casually as she could, so anyone looking wouldn't remark on it, she turned her head. The dark-haired guy who'd called her Jones was standing amidst a group of frankly thuggish-looking young men, staring at her across the quad. Subtlety forgotten, she whipped her head back around and stood there stiffly.

It was too much to expect her new friends not to notice.

"What's wrong?" Kaye asked.

Freya shook her head and tried to control her expression, but Gev said, "You look like you've seen a ghost."

"It's nothing," Freya muttered.

Kaye looked past her. "Is it the island of misfit boys?"

"The what?"

"That little hill over there where the xenos hang out," Kaye said.

"Xenos?"

Sandrew laughed humorlessly. "Yeah, we got us a bad infestation. You don't want to mess with them."

"Except maybe Dan Corvi," Jin said. "I'd mess around with him any day."

Sandrew shot her a dour look. "No one said anything about messing *around*."

Jin responded, but Freya had tuned them out. She was no longer looking in the dark-haired guy's direction, but her peripheral vision insisted that he was still watching her.

This is ridiculous, she told herself. *Get a grip.*

She stood there pretending to listen to her new friends, when all the while her mind was spinning in a different direction altogether. What *was* it about the guy that provoked such a strange gut reaction? He was attractive enough, but she'd never been drawn to the bad boy type before. Not that she was drawn to him. In fact, her instinct was to bolt whenever she saw him. She'd felt nearly the exact same way in the presence of Trevor Segal, the young man at her last school who'd taken such an interest in her that she and her mother had been forced to run. The whole thing baffled and unnerved her. Out of necessity, paranoia had become a big part of her life, but up until lately she'd been able to balance it with reason.

Thankfully, the bell rang, and she managed to avoid running into the dark-haired guy until the one class they had together. As she filed out of the locker room with the other students, she found herself walking directly behind him. His gym shirt read, "Corvi," and she realized he was the xeno Jin had commented on.

Dan Corvi.

Out on the back field, she and the rest of her classmates milled about waiting for Mr. Gillan to make an appearance. Freya maneuvered for a spot that put most of them between her and Dan.

Figuring Mr. Gillan would send them to run a lap again, she bent to stretch her hamstrings. When she straightened up, Dan was standing next to her.

"Hi," he said. His eyes under thick, devilishly slanted eyebrows, were green.

She swallowed against a sudden lump in her throat. "Hey."

"Didn't mean to freak you out yesterday." He held out his hand. "I'm Dan."

She halfway expected something strange to happen when their fingers touched, but it didn't. She shook his hand and let go quickly. "Freya."

"Where you from?"

She opened her mouth but was spared having to lie when Mr. Gillan showed up and sent them off on their warmup lap. Afterward, she ended up on Dan's basketball team. Before her martial arts training, basketball held no appeal for her. It had always struck her as such an intrusive sport, as the players elbowed each other jockeying for position. Karate and kickboxing had forced her to abandon her aversion for close combat sports. She still sucked at sinking baskets, but she was no longer afraid to get her hands on the ball.

Not that anyone actually passed it to her, even when she was in position to make a basket. There were three guys on her team, each apparently a diehard ball hog. Even Dan, who'd been so eager to get her attention, hardly seemed to notice her once they started playing. Normally, Freya wasn't the type to wait around for someone to include her, but months of hiding – of staying under the radar – had taken its toll. She was content to let the guys dominate the game.

Then Mr. Gillan wandered over and called out, "Let's hear some chatter, girls! Your teammates don't know you're open unless you tell them."

Freya exchanged a look of disgust with the other girl on her team. "Yeah, because they can't actually *see* us."

"Maybe if we took our tops off," the girl suggested. She had lightly freckled skin and curly reddish hair pulled into a ponytail. Her gym shirt read, "Stanton."

Freya laughed. "That might work."

She turned back to the game just in time to see Dan attempt a shot. With his arms raised, the sleeves of his gym shirt slipped enough to give her a glimpse of his xenograft. Just the sight of the scales wrapped around his upper arm set Freya's heart to racing. She averted her eyes and pressed a hand to her chest, taking a few deep breaths.

"You okay?" Stanton asked.

Freya nodded, her gaze involuntarily finding Dan. She might not understand what it was about him that made her feel so threatened, but she did know one thing: it made her angry.

Dan glanced over, catching her off guard before she could mask the resentment on her face. The last thing she expected was for him to look like someone had punched him in the gut. One of their teammates bounced a pass to him, but he didn't even see the ball coming. It glanced off his elbow right into the waiting hands of Stanton, who passed it to Freya. She dribbled it to the basket, but the other team was all over her, so she passed it back to Stanton. With apparent ease, Stanton spun to avoid a player, bounced the ball twice, and then sank a jump shot.

23

All the while, Dan stood there, arms hanging loosely at his sides. The other two male players on Freya's team high-fived Stanton.

For the rest of the game, Dan seemed to be doing everything in his power to avoid Freya.

Which was fine by her.

Chapter Six

After school, Dan met up with Bass for the walk home, keeping a wary eye out for that Freya girl. As soon as he and Bass were clear of the exodus of students, he said, "There's something really strange going on."

"Oh, yeah?"

"'Member how I told you I liked the way Freya Jones smelled?"

"Her first name is Freya?" Bass asked.

"Yes," Dan replied impatiently.

"Uh, yeah, I remember. It was yesterday. That'd be pretty sad if I already forgot something–"

"Bass."

"What?" Bass looked at him, and then raised his eyebrows. "You look freaked."

"That's because I *am*. I think she wears some kind of perfume that, I don't know, attracts me."

"What, like pheromones?"

Dan nodded. "I get seriously disturbed urges when I'm around her."

Bass laughed. "Urges?"

"Yuk it up."

"Sorry." Bass pressed his lips together in an effort to lose the smile. "What kind of urges? The usual?"

"No, that's just it. I wouldn't think twice about it if I was just attracted to her. This is...different."

They jaywalked across the street. "Different how?"

"I don't know! Like I want to–" Dan stopped himself from saying, "bite her," because he knew how it sounded. Bass would think he'd lost his marbles.

"You want to what?"

Dan sighed. "Never mind."

25

Of course Bass wasn't going to just let the subject drop. "Is it something illegal?"

Dan bent his head back and looked up at the cloudless sky. Reluctantly, he said, "It's like I'm starving to death and she's the only food in the fridge."

"So you want to…eat her?" Normally, Bass would have emphasized the double entendre in his words, but the tentative way he said it told Dan he was genuinely trying to understand the problem.

"Yeah."

Bass curled his upper lip under, displaying his teeth. "In a vampire kind of way, or more like a werewolf?"

Dan glared at him in disbelief. "What's the difference? No, don't answer that."

"Look, maybe you have anemia or something. A physical reason for wanting to chow down on girls."

"Girl. Just one. But why her?"

They'd arrived in the parking lot of the apartment complex.

"No idea," Bass said. "I doubt it's her perfume, though. If it was, Wade would have made an afternoon snack out of her yesterday for sure."

Dan let out a little laugh of agreement. Then he caught sight of Freya. "Here she comes. I'm outta here."

"See you tomorrow," Bass said.

Dan waved absently in Bass' direction and walked quickly towards his building. He didn't want to get caught in Freya's sphere of influence, whether it was her scent causing his reaction or not.

In his apartment, his dad was sitting on the couch watching holovision. That's pretty much what Randolph Corvi did all day, every day. At yesterday's appointment, the doctor had stressed that his age and the fact that he hadn't been in a coma for very long were good indicators of eventual recovery, but that his persistent amnesia was troubling. Once again, Dan was told that the doctor couldn't offer a definitive prognosis. "Wait and see," was sure getting old.

He took a seat next to his dad, who was watching the governor give a speech on the news. His dad seemed to be completely absorbed by it, not even acknowledging Dan's presence. A year ago, Dan wouldn't have dreamed of asking him about his problem, but now he wished more than anything that it was an option.

After a few minutes, he went into his room and flopped onto the bed. He took out his holophone to check his mail and opened one from the research company that had given him his xenograft. He didn't really feel like completing the weekly survey, but since it only ever took a few minutes, he went ahead and did so. Twenty bucks was twenty bucks.

The questions were always the same. He could tell they were designed to determine if he was experiencing any side-effects to the graft. His answer choices were "Yes," "No," and "Not Sure." He'd never checked anything but the "No" box to any of the questions, but this time, he hesitated at one of them.

"Have you experienced any new and/or unusual compulsions?" he read aloud, and then laughed. "You mean like wanting to gnaw on the new girl?"

His initial reaction was to lie, because he suspected if he admitted to it, he'd be called into the clinic to talk to a doctor. Then he asked himself if that would be such a bad thing. Something was definitely wrong. He didn't know for sure it had anything to do with his graft, but it was making him miserable. He checked the "Yes" box, and a question he'd never seen before popped up.

"Are you experiencing aggression?" He almost checked "Not Sure," but decided on "Yes."

An additional question popped up. "Is this aggression directed at only one person?"

Dan frowned. *How'd they know?* He answered "Yes."

Another question appeared. This one was multiple choice. "Check all that apply. A. This person is male. B. This person is female. C. This person lives near me. D. This person is a co-worker. E. This person attends the same school. F. This person is a stranger I encountered once."

He couldn't fathom why they needed the information, but he checked B, C and E.

After that, he spent the next hour on homework, and then decided to go work out before his mom got home. Their apartment complex was no great shakes, but it did boast a small outdoor swimming pool with a hot tub that was usually closed due to some bacterial hazard or another, and a large malodorous room containing ancient exercise equipment that was generously referred to as the Fitness Center.

The reason he liked the place was because he usually had it to himself. This afternoon there was one other person using the equipment, but ten minutes into Dan's circuit training routine, the guy left. A few minutes after that, the door opened and Freya Jones came in, dressed in shorts and a tank top, and carrying a bottle of water, a small white towel, and a pair of boxing gloves. She caught sight of him, and even from across the room he saw her recoil slightly. He fully expected her to turn tail and leave, but she lifted her chin and walked over to the duct-tape-covered heavy punching bag hanging in the corner.

For the next twenty minutes, while he jogged on the treadmill and listened to his workout playlist, he surreptitiously watched her. She had a very simple routine consisting of one-two, one-two jabs, followed by one kick to the side of the bag with the top of her foot, alternating legs after the jabs. Several times she stopped to rest, sipping from her water bottle and blotting her face and chest with the towel.

As much as he was tempted to extend his workout so he could continue gawking at her, he decided it would be in his best interest to vacate the premises, especially since noticing that the intensity of her workout made her tank top partially transparent where it clung to her torso. While before his attraction to her had been strictly carnivorous, now her lightly muscled, yet feminine body had stirred more carnal urges.

Fearing his own reaction should he happen to catch her scent, he left the Fitness Center with a good deal of self-preserving haste.

Chapter Seven

Freya's first two days of school had been exhausting, what with her tough classes, the weirdness with Dan Corvi, and especially the constant stress of pretending to be someone she wasn't. It was her third day and she still had that anxious feeling that at any moment she'd be exposed as a fraud. Her new friends, with their bottomless curiosity and unrelentingly caustic yet cheerful banter, didn't help matters. Before school, she'd fended off some particularly probing questions through vagueness and deflection, but she suspected those tactics wouldn't work much longer. Eventually, she'd have to open up – or at least seem to.

In the locker room before gym class, Freya angled her body so her backside was shielded by the open door of her locker and stripped off her jeans. The two-inch by four-inch xenograft she'd gotten as part of the medical research study that had ruined her life had been placed on her lower back. She'd developed lots of different approaches in order to hide it from the casual observer.

Out on the basketball courts, Mr. Gillan divided the class into teams again, placing Dan Corvi on the next court over from Freya. Without his disturbing presence, Freya relaxed to the point that she almost enjoyed the game – until she noticed Sandrew taking holos with his phone from the sideline.

She abandoned the game and walked over to him.

"What are you doing?" she asked.

Sandrew lowered his phone. "What's it look like?"

"I don't give you permission to take my holo. If you have any, please delete them. Now."

"It's for yearbook." Sandrew shrugged, like there was nothing he could do about it.

"Miss Jones!" Mr. Gillan called. "Back in the game."

Freya maintained eye contact with Sandrew as she walked backwards towards the court. "Delete them. *Please.*"

A crease formed between Sandrew's brows, but he bent his head and seemed to be doing something with his phone. Freya hoped he was honoring her wishes and deleting any holos he'd taken of her. The last thing she needed was her image getting out there. If it did, and if the killers found her because of it, she and her mother would die a tragic, "accidental" death, just like all the others.

After school, she saw Sandrew again, standing with the rest of the gang by the flagpole, as usual. She headed straight for him.

"Hi," Jin said, a lilt of surprise in her voice. "Normally you don't stray from the shortest path off school property."

Freya smiled. "Well, today I thought I'd have a chat with Sandrew before leaving."

"About the holo thing?" Gev asked.

From their faces, everyone present seemed to know what Gev was referring to.

"Uh, yeah…that," Freya said, as a sick feeling began brewing in her gut.

Sandrew glanced around, and once he'd verified that no outsiders were close enough to hear, said, "Instead of deleting the holos I took of you, I ran a search for visually similar facial holos on the interweb. Who are you really?"

Freya took a deep breath and let it out slowly, but her attempt to keep her reaction from showing must have failed miserably.

"Wow," Gev said, studying Freya's face. "I've read about it, but I've never actually seen anyone go pale as a ghost before."

"Is she gonna pass out?" Cindy sidled closer like she was putting herself into position to catch Freya if she did.

"You *do* know there's a reward for information on your whereabouts, right?" Sandrew's brown eyes narrowed slightly, as if he were avidly anticipating Freya's response.

Freya hadn't known that but wasn't surprised. Despite her best efforts to appear unaffected, tears filled her eyes. "I don't know what you're talking about."

"Quit, you guys." Jin placed a gentle hand on Freya's shoulder. "I told them it was a mistake."

"Or maybe you have a doppelganger," Gev suggested.

Sandrew looked unconvinced. "Unless you take into account her reaction just now."

Freya cursed her bad luck in meeting this particular group of kids. Sandrew was way too astute for her to convince him to drop it, but maybe copping to a partial truth combined with playing the sympathy card would buy her some time.

"It wasn't a doppelganger or a mistake," she said. "There are really bad people looking for me and my mom."

"Who are they? The people looking for you." Cindy glanced around like she would defend Freya to the death if anyone messed with her.

"I don't know. Just that if they find me, I'm dead. My mom, too."

"You honestly have no idea why this is happening?" Jin asked.

Freya's gaze dropped to the ground, and Sandrew said, "Oh, she knows."

"I have a general idea," Freya snapped, "but I don't know who they are, or specifically *why* they want us all dead."

Sandrew tilted his head. "'Us all?' Who besides you and your mother?"

"I can't tell you. Please just let it go."

"So is your name really Freya?" he asked, completely ignoring her plea. "Because the site with the reward is calling you Amanda."

It was clear he wasn't going to back off, and he'd done exactly what Ryan had warned her and her mother not to do: search the interweb for information on her. If the bad guys' technical skills were as sophisticated as Ryan suspected, they'd be able to find Sandrew through his holophone.

Freya decided to cut her losses. "Just give me enough time to get home and warn my mom before you collect the reward, okay?"

"I could totally use the money, but until I have all the facts, I'm not going to be the one to turn you in," Sandrew said.

"The *facts* could get you killed." Freya lifted a shaking hand to brush a stray lock of hair out of her eyes. She wanted to leave but was terrified Sandrew would contact the bad guys the minute she turned her back on him.

"Tell you what," he said. "I'll text them and ask who they are."

"You think they'll tell you? More likely, they'll kidnap and torture you for information."

He laughed. "Melodramatic much?"

"They killed seventeen people that I know of. That sound melodramatic?"

He lifted a shoulder. "Yeah."

It was like talking to a brick wall, but she didn't blame him for being skeptical. None of them had any reason to believe her. She looked at each of their faces before saying, "It was nice meeting all of you," and turning away. Sandrew's hand shot out and he grasped her upper arm.

31

"Don't go. I won't tell anyone, I swear. I'll delete the pictures."

Freya closed her eyes for a moment before looking into his eyes intensely. "You're asking me to trust all of you with *my life*. If one of you slips up and says something…"

"We won't," Cindy said.

Jin swept a hand to indicate the others. "We've been friends since grade school. We all have secrets, but none of us have ever blabbed."

"Any of your secrets life or death?" Freya asked.

Jin and the others looked at Gev, who bit her lip. "Maybe."

Freya's gaze drifted upward, where dark clouds had gathered in the sky. They really were nice kids, and she wanted to trust them, but there was too much at stake. In order to get Sandrew to let go of her arm though, she said, "Okay. I'll see you tomorrow."

Sandrew's eyes narrowed, but he released her.

As Freya strode away, she reached into her backpack and found the holophone Ryan had given her for emergencies.

Chapter Eight

Dan watched Freya walk across the street, wondering what she and her new friends had been talking about. Sandrew was kind of squirrelly, but not a bad guy. Still, when he'd grabbed Freya's arm, Dan had to suppress the urge to stalk over and forcibly remove his hand.

Wade leaned into his field of view. "Danny boy. You listening?"

Dan turned his attention back to Wade, who'd been trying to interest him in going on a salvage run. "Sorry. You said it was an underground shopping mall?"

"Supposed to be, but it never got finished. It was Mad Eye headquarters until they abandoned it."

"Wait a minute. You talking about Edgemere?" Dan asked. "That place was a death trap *before* the riots."

"Rumors," Wade replied. "To keep people away."

"You think the Mad Eye left anything?" Bass asked.

"Dunno, but my dad heard they vacated in a hurry. Some kind of chemical spill."

"Where's Mick?" Dan asked.

"Getting something from Chem Lab," Wade said with a suggestive lift of his eyebrows, but Dan's attention had already wandered, caught by a police car driving past the school, not an unusual sight in this neighborhood. While the others discussed the salvage run, he watched as the police car stopped behind a black SUV parked at the far end of the street. Then a white van blocked his view by pulling up in front of the school in a no park zone. Dan almost turned back to his friends' conversation, but then a pregnant woman with dark sunglasses and a black scarf draped over her head got out of the van. The van's driver, a big man with a salt and pepper crew cut, got out, too. He and the woman walked over to a group of kids sitting on the city bus stop bench. The woman activated her holophone and showed them something. Dan couldn't see the holo, but whatever it was, a couple of the kids shook their heads. The man and woman then headed for the next group of kids, which happened to be Sandrew and company.

Dan looked around for Freya. She'd stopped at the corner and was staring in the direction of the police car. Then her head turned towards the occupants of the white van, and the alarm on her face was evident even from a distance.

"There he is," Wade said, pulling Dan's attention away from Freya's drama.

Mick was striding through the school's main doors, making a beeline for them.

When he was a few yards away, he held up several of the emergency gas masks Dan had seen hanging on the wall in Chemistry class.

"Got 'em," he said, "but we should vamoose. I think Ms. Jackson saw me."

Wade socked Dan lightly on the arm. "You coming?"

Dan shook his head. "Nah."

"Your loss. Bass?"

"Sure," Bass said. "But I gotta stop off at home first." He lifted his backpack.

The three of them headed for the school parking lot, but Dan hardly noticed. The man and woman from the white van were showing the holo to Sandrew and his friends, all of whom looked highly intimidated. Curiosity got the better of him, and before he knew it, he'd walked over.

"Hey, guys," he said, like he chatted with them all the time.

Sandrew's face was so tense his lips barely moved. "Dan."

The woman held out her holophone. In a lightly accented voice, she asked, "Have you seen this girl?"

The holo was of Freya, but with longer, slightly darker hair.

Dan shrugged. "Nope."

The man inclined his head. "Thanks. You kids have a nice day."

As he and his companion moved to the next group of loitering students, a sprinkling of raindrops began to fall.

"How'd they know?" Gev's words were hushed.

Sandrew shot her a look that Dan interpreted as a warning.

"Who are they?" Dan asked.

"Said they were cops," Sandrew replied.

Dan glanced over at the police car at the end of the block. A uniformed officer was standing next to the driver's side door of the van, talking to the driver through the open window. Dan shifted his gaze to the white van. It was older, nondescript. "You see a badge?"

Sandrew shook his head.

"Then they weren't cops. Why are they looking for Freya?"

"Keep it down," Jin snapped. "If you knew the holo was Freya, why didn't you say so?"

Dan was about to answer, but Sandrew said, "They're going inside."

As soon as the man and woman passed through the weapons detector, a shrill alarm sounded. They ignored it and kept on going. Dan looked at the real police officer, who didn't react. He was either too far away to hear it or was ignoring it.

"Oh, my God," Sandrew said. "We gotta warn her."

"About what?" Dan's patience was growing thin.

"That some sketchy people are looking for her," Cindy said. "*Jeez.*"

"Anyone got her number?" When Jin's question garnered only negative responses, she sighed in frustration.

"I know where she lives," Dan said, although technically he didn't know what apartment it was.

"Where?" Sandrew demanded.

Dan looked at him blandly. "Tell me why those people are looking for her."

Sandrew glared up at him for several seconds. "We promised we wouldn't."

"Promised who?"

"Freya, you idiot!" Cindy cried.

Dan had no idea why they were so concerned, but they were clearly on the verge of panic.

"She lives in my building," he said. "I'll tell her." Although from the look on her face earlier, he figured she already knew.

"Hurry." Gev tossed a worried look over her shoulder at the school. "Candace Beckett is an aide in the office. She'll give them her address for sure."

Dan had gotten maybe ten yards away when Sandrew called out, "Could you maybe go a little faster?"

Obligingly, Dan increased his pace. When he got to the corner, he saw that Freya had almost reached the apartment complex. If she went into the building, he'd have to knock on doors to find her, assuming she even bothered to answer. He'd just decided to break into a run when Wade pulled up next to him in the jeep.

"Want a ride?"

Dan jumped into the back next to Bass and slammed the door. Within thirty seconds, they'd arrived in time for him to see the lobby door close behind Freya.

He leapt out of the jeep and ran after her. In the stairwell, he heard her rapid footfalls on the cement steps. There was no point calling out to her; she'd probably just go faster.

He took the steps two at a time, reaching the third floor landing just as she was opening the door to the hallway. She spun around, fists raised, and he flashed on her kickboxing workout the other day. Her intensity was beginning to make sense.

"Whoa." He raised his hands. "Your friends wanted me to tell you someone's looking for you."

She released a shaky breath and said dismissively, "Yeah. Thanks."

He followed her into the hallway, but went straight to his apartment, where he took his time unlocking the door so he could surreptitiously watch her. She entered the apartment two doors down from his. Last he knew, it had been occupied by a xeno named Mouse, and since he would have noticed if Mouse had moved out, he assumed Freya was staying with her.

After the excitement of chasing after her, it was a bit of a letdown to go into his apartment. His dad was watching the news again. Dan made his way to the living room window and opened the blinds.

The white van was cruising slowly up the street. He watched until it passed out of view. From this vantage point, he couldn't see if it turned into the complex parking lot, but he figured it had.

Now what? he thought.

Chapter Nine

Freya, too, had gone straight to the window, looking out through the rain-streaked glass. When she saw the white van, her first instinct was to rush headlong out of the apartment. She grabbed her backpack, but logic managed to intrude upon her adrenaline-saturated brain. Leaving by the front door meant she'd likely run into her pursuers in the lobby or stairwell. The other obvious choice was to bang on Dan Corvi's door and beg him to hide her – but he scared her almost as much as the occupants of the white van.

She stood in the middle of the living room, frantically thinking. On the walk home, she'd called her mother, who hadn't picked up. Her mom was scheduled to work the swing shift at Bluto's, so she was probably on the bus. Freya had left a message, and then immediately called her cousin Ryan. He'd told her he was on his way and that she should stay put, but now she knew there was no way he'd get here in time. Assuming the bad guys knocked on her door, she could ignore it and hope they went away, but something about the big guy with the crew cut told her he wouldn't hesitate to break in.

She went back to the window. The fire escape looked rickety, but it was her best option.

She unzipped her backpack and dumped the contents – schoolbooks and her binder – onto the couch. Then she dug through the black garbage bag with all of her belongings in it, grabbing things she might need willy-nilly and stuffing them into the backpack.

At the window, she took a deep breath that did nothing to calm her racing pulse and opened it, tossing her backpack out onto the fire escape. She climbed out, conscious of her footing on the wet metal grating. She'd always been intimidated by heights, and by the time she reached the sliding ladder at the bottom level, she was sure the climb had bumped her intimidation into full-blown acrophobia. She wanted to kiss the ground when the soles of her boots finally made contact with it.

She had no destination in mind other than to disappear – and fast. She looked up and down the street and decided she'd be too exposed to stick to the sidewalk. Across the road, a narrow alley between buildings looked promising. At the very least, she could hide behind the rusty dumpster, where she would have full view of the apartment complex. Maybe once the people in the white van left, it would be safe to return to Mouse's apartment.

She stepped into the street, but before she'd gotten halfway across, she heard the screech of tires and looked fearfully to her right. It was that xeno Wade, driving his jeep like a maniac. He stopped in the middle of the road and the back door opened. Dan Corvi called out, "They're right behind us! Get in!"

Freya didn't trust him, but it only took a split second to acknowledge that he and his friends were the lesser of two evils. He scooted closer to Bass and she climbed into the jeep next to him, backpack on her lap. Wade hit the electrigas pedal before the door had fully shut behind her. She pulled the seatbelt and clicked it, all the while looking out the dirty back window. They got to the end of the block without any sign of the white van. She was beginning to think Dan and his friends were playing some kind of sick prank on her when the van shot out of the parking lot.

Dan turned to her. "Stop looking. They'll see you."

She faced front and stared down at her backpack.

"Are they following us?" Bass asked.

"Let's find out." Wade took a right and then an immediate left. After a minute or so, he looked in the rearview mirror and said with obvious relish, "Yep. We've definitely got a tail."

"Drive to the police station," Bass said.

"No!" Freya exclaimed. "No police. Please."

"Whatever you say." Wade sped up, taking a sharp turn into a supermarket parking lot. The jeep bounced over the speed bumps. Horns honked as Wade cut off other drivers, and a pedestrian he nearly side-swiped shouted obscenities.

"So what'd you do?" The question from the shaggy-haired guy in the passenger seat was directed at Freya.

"Nothing." She grabbed the door armrest and braced herself as the jeep turned sharply back onto the road.

"Huh," the guy said. "People in the habit of chasing you for nothing?"

Normally, she'd be ready with a quick retort, but fear had emptied her head of glibness.

"Leave her alone, Mick," Dan said.

A look of disbelief crossed Mick's face. "You don't wanna know who we're running from – and why?"

Freya silently acknowledged that he had a point, but now was not the time to attempt an explanation. Wade drove them up and over a curb, through a large gap in a chain link fence, and across a field, tires fishtailing through the mud. On the far side of the field, he drove down a narrow gravel lane between rows of derelict trailer homes.

"Whoever they were," he said as the jeep merged into traffic on a busy boulevard, "I think we lost them."

Freya's next thought was for Ryan – how he was about to arrive at the apartment to find her gone. She dug her holophone out of her backpack and called him.

He answered on the first ring, and from the angle of the holo, was using the dash cam in his sedan.

"Where are you?" he asked before she could speak.

"Driving with…friends. They came after us, but we lost them."

Mick had twisted in his seat to see the holo. "Wait a minute," he said. "I recognize that guy."

Wade glanced around and scowled before turning back to the road. "Knuckles."

Freya sat very still next to Dan. She knew little about Ryan's undercover work with the XIA but did know his xeno name was Knuckles because of the alligator hide that used to be grafted across the knuckles of both hands. Belatedly, it occurred to her that she should have made the call voice only.

"That's right," Ryan responded, his tone cold. "You boys best not mess with my cousin."

"Freya's your cousin?" Mick looked at her with what she interpreted as predatory interest, and the impression only grew stronger when Bass said under his breath, "Ohhh no."

Ryan ignored Mick and repeated his earlier question. "Where are you exactly?"

Freya opened her mouth to respond, but Wade said, "We're on our way to visit my dad in the hospital. You remember Cerberus, right, Knuckles?"

Ryan's face gave nothing away, but Freya sensed his irritation as he said, "It was his choice to take me on. Now tell me where you are."

Mick reached through the holo image and snatched Freya's phone out of her hand. "We're on our way to a private party with your sweet little cousin," he said, then disconnected.

"Give it back!" Freya demanded.

Mick acted like he didn't see her outstretched hand, instead tucking her holophone into his pants pocket. "You'll get it later. After your scumbag cousin has a little time to worry."

"So. Freya." Wade met her eyes in the rearview mirror. "I assume the people chasing you are xenos? Someone else with a grudge against Knuckles?"

"This has nothing to do with him," she said. "Could you please just drop me off here?"

"What, on the side of the road? I'm not gonna strand you in the rain." Wade's voice dripped faux sincerity. "Hanging with us for a couple hours isn't too much to ask after we saved your bacon, is it?"

Dan, previously quick to defend her, stared expressionlessly out the front windshield, but then he nudged her with his elbow, a subtle movement she interpreted as a warning. Whatever Ryan had done to Wade's dad "Cerberus" had clearly agitated them. Her best bet would be to play along until they arrived at whatever destination Wade had in mind.

"You're right," she said. "And...thank you."

"You're welcome," Wade replied. "Now that wasn't so hard, was it?"

Chapter Ten

Sitting next to Freya for the remainder of the drive was pure torture for Dan, and he sensed that being in such close proximity to him wasn't fun for her either. She'd not only withdrawn from further conversation but had retreated from any physical contact with him. Her knees were clamped tightly together, and her entire body leaned towards the door. She gazed bleakly out the window.

As for Dan, he was tormented by the insistent urges he felt for her. When Bass opened a bag of potato chips and offered him a handful, he gobbled them down as if they could somehow assuage his strange hunger.

It didn't take long to figure out that Wade was headed for their original destination: Rockaway Peninsula, location of the infamous Edgemere, abandoned now except for the ghosts that were said to haunt the place. What had Wade said? Something about a chemical spill. That was why Mick had stolen the gas masks from Chem Lab, so they'd be safe to enter the contaminated underground mall.

Not that "safe" was a word Dan would use to describe any salvage run.

The thousands of homes and businesses destroyed during the riots had provided a plethora of opportunity for scavengers. Scrap metal paid big, but months after the riots, the bounty had dried up, making it harder to find the good stuff. A salvage run to former Mad Eye territory was flat-out dangerous. Dan would have hesitated even if Freya wasn't being dragged along for the ride.

The view out the window had changed from hectic city bustle to squalid urban sprawl. The rain fell more heavily the closer they got to the ocean. The jeep's windshield wipers squeaked industriously across the glass, punctuated by the occasional rumble of thunder. When they drove across the bridge, there were no other cars in sight.

On the far side of the bay, Wade turned a few times and then slowed down to navigate through and around puddles in the depressions where the asphalt had crumbled away, or where wind-blown sand had formed dunes in the road. What Dan could see of their surroundings seemed like something out of a post-apocalyptic movie. The land, once cleared to lay roads for a new community that had never seen completion, was actively being reclaimed by nature.

The final turn revealed their destination – a huge, unfinished structure low to the ground – a vast slab of concrete peppered with tumbleweeds that had gotten caught on its rusty steel girders.

As Wade drove alongside the slab, the ground sloped downward, partially exposing the corner of the underground structure. He turned and drove right up to the open end of an enormous biopolycrete drainage pipe; the only visible entrance to the place. He put the jeep in park. Its headlights cut through the rain but were unable to penetrate very far into the blackness within the pipe.

"You bring flashlights?" Bass asked.

"Of course," Wade said, but didn't get out of the jeep.

After a brief silence that gave Dan the impression Wade was reconsidering the plan, Bass seized the opportunity to be the bravest amongst them and opened his door. He walked cockily to the back of the vehicle and lifted the hatch.

Dan unfastened his seat belt and moved away from Freya to occupy the spot Bass had vacated. Wade looked inquiringly at him.

"I'll stay with her," Dan said.

Wade let out a lecherous little chuckle. "Figured you would."

He shut off the engine and pocketed the keys before reaching across Mick to open the glove box. Dan wasn't surprised when Wade took out a handgun, which he tucked into the waistband of his pants at the small of his back before joining Bass out in the rain. Mick hooked a finger through the rubber straps on the gas masks and got out, too. Dan and Freya watched as they fit the gas masks over their faces. Mick and Bass lit the way into the pipe with the flashlights while Wade carried an ax in one hand and the toolbox they would need to strip Edgemere of any and all recyclable materials they might find in the other.

"Give me your holophone," Freya said as soon as the others had disappeared into the pipe.

"It's at home. I kinda left in a hurry."

She seemed disappointed, but then gazed into his eyes intently. "Why did you help me?"

Dan broke eye contact to look down at his clasped hands. "I don't know."

"Yes, you do."

He shook his head. "Seriously, I don't. There's something about you. It's hard to explain."

"You're not...*scared* of me, are you?" she asked.

Surprised, he looked up at her. "Of course not. Why?"

It was her turn to break eye contact. "Never mind. How long do you think they'll be? I really need to call my mom."

"Don't worry, alright? I won't let anything–" he stopped as he caught a brief glint of something. He turned his head. Out the back window, he saw headlights approaching.

"We've got company."

Discussion wasn't necessary. Dan opened his door and slid out, followed closely by Freya, who clutched her backpack to her chest. He shut the door quietly, glad that Wade had parked at an angle that put the jeep between them and the newcomers. There was no way they wouldn't be seen if they attempted to enter the drainage pipe, so he took Freya's arm and urged her towards a thick copse of evergreen bushes nearby. They ran, bent over to reduce their visibility. He glanced behind him at the exact moment a flash of lightning lit their immediate surroundings, and saw the white van pulling up next to the jeep.

A narrow path led them into the midst of what turned out to be holly bushes. It was gloomy under cover of the leaves, but not dark enough to hide a cleared space with what appeared to be a collapsed tent and miscellaneous discarded items scattered around. Dan had no desire to investigate what had obviously been a campground for some homeless person or persons. They were shielded from the direct effects of the rain, but plenty of water dripped from the leaves, and they were drenched in no time.

He couldn't see the vehicles through the foliage, but he heard the sound of a car door slamming. There was nothing to do but listen...and wait. Freya's wool coat looked far from waterproof and she began to shiver, shoulders shaking from the cold. He went over to the campsite and looked down at it. The tent's camouflage pattern was faded and stained, probably from having been out in the elements for some time. The fabric was torn, filthy, and smelled like a combination of wet dog and urine. As shelter went, it was a non-starter.

He moved back to stand next to Freya, whose teeth had begun to chatter delicately. "Tent's trashed," he whispered. "I'd give you my hoodie, but I'm soaked, too."

A look of annoyed realization crossed her face, and she unzipped her backpack. She rummaged around inside, finally pulling out a compact umbrella.

"Ah," he said quietly. "Holding out on me, huh?"

She opened the umbrella, but only partially. Her comment, "It's kind of bright," was an understatement. The pink, orange and red floral pattern was positively psychedelic.

"Oh, yeah, that'll work," he mocked, taking the umbrella and examining it with a twist of his lips. "Everyone in a ten-mile radius will see us, but we'll be dry. You got any fireworks or air-raid sirens in that backpack?"

She glared up at him. "I had thirty seconds to pack and no way of knowing I'd end up stuck out–"

Dan shushed her mid-sentence. "You hear that?"

Raised voices echoed faintly. He imagined a confrontation between the big guy in the van and Wade, who was always looking for a fight. Just when he'd almost convinced himself Wade wouldn't do anything stupid, he heard a sharp report that could only be gunfire. He put an arm around Freya, pulling her down into a crouch next to him. "We either stay here and hope they don't see us, or we run."

She was looking fixedly into the underbrush near the tent, her only response a faint, "Um…"

He followed her gaze. Standing partially concealed not ten feet away was a large dog, mangy, thin, and growling now that Dan made eye contact with it.

Chapter Eleven

Freya's mother was a veterinarian, which had exposed Freya from a young age to many animals. Ellie had schooled her daughter ad nauseam about what to do if confronted by a threatening dog. Freya grabbed her backpack and stood so she wasn't facing the dog.

"Get up. Don't look at it. Stay calm," she said quietly.

Dan did as she asked, moving to stand between her and the dog. She leaned forward to keep it in her peripheral vision as she unzipped a pocket on the front of her backpack. Inside was one of the "emergency" protein bars her mother always insisted she have on hand at any given time. She gently removed it, and then slipped her hand through the backpack's straps, hanging it on her forearm to free both hands. As she tore the wrapper, more sounds came from inside Edgemere: shouting, clanging, and most frightening, a few more gunshots.

The dog had taken several steps closer, teeth bared, and hackles raised. The last thing Freya wanted to do was draw any attention to them from outside the thicket, but the immediate threat was the dog. She spoke softly in a high voice, "Hey, puppy. Want a treat?" Then she tossed the protein bar towards the dog. It landed a few feet away. For a moment, she thought the dog would ignore it – a very bad sign – but then she saw its head come up and turn as it scented the offering. The dog, stiff-legged, walked to the protein bar.

"We need to leave," she said, taking a small step to the side. "Slowly."

There was only one path and they couldn't take it without being seen if anyone was still in the van, so she forced her way between two bushes, using her backpack as a shield against the spiny leaves. Thick branches slowed her progress to only a few feet into the foliage, preventing Dan from following. Renewed growling told her the protein bar gambit had been unsuccessful.

45

She looked behind her. Dan's soaking wet hair hung in his eyes, rivulets streaming down his face like tears.

"Tell it to lie down," she said. "Firmly."

Before Dan could comply, the dog lunged, snarling and barking, but Dan pressed the button on the shaft of the umbrella, and it popped fully open right in the dog's face. Freya, discarding caution, turned back to the wall of branches and leaves and plowed forward, heedless of the spines catching on her coat and hair. The umbrella must have startled the dog, because all barking stopped just as an engine roared beyond the grove of holly trees. Surrounded on all sides by foliage, Freya spotted grey sky up ahead and fought her way through the last of the bushes, stumbling into the open just in time to see the jeep's taillights disappear around a bend.

A split second after Dan reached her side, he grabbed her and pulled her partially back among the branches as the white van shot into view. The driver turned to follow the jeep. When the van was gone, she stood and stared after it, but only for a moment, because Dan took her elbow. "We need to put some space between us and that mutt." He steered her towards what was left of the road, but she shook him off.

"We shouldn't go that way." She nodded in the direction the vehicles had gone. "They might realize I'm not in the jeep and circle back."

"There's another bridge across the bay that way." He gestured in the opposite direction.

She scanned the terrain, hoping to see signs of civilization, but there was only sand, sky and the decaying roads. Even the scrubby plant life and mournfully crying seabirds seemed to have carved out the bleakest of existences.

Dan walked fast and Freya kept up without protest, eager to get as far away from Edgemere as possible. The exercise warmed her except for her extremities – fingers, toes, ears and nose – which ached from the cold. She balled her hands into fists in her pockets, her gaze trained on the uneven ground as she walked. The rain fell with no sign of letting up. Their course took them parallel to the coastline on the left, and on the right, the bare bones foundations of whole streets of housing that had been flattened by hurricane Poppy years ago. After what felt like a miserable long time, she saw a few standing houses in the distance.

They hadn't spoken a word to each other during the cold, wet trek, but with the prospect of shelter, she broke the silence. "Probably not a very good neighborhood."

"Definitely not a good neighborhood. This entire area was trashed during the riots."

"I thought that was Coney Island."

46

"Here, too. They burned just about everything."

She squinted at the houses apprehensively, trying to see them better through the rain and haze. The closer she and Dan got, the stronger her misgivings, as the extent of the destruction became more apparent. Unlike the houses destroyed by Poppy, evidence of which had been mostly obliterated over time by the environment, the remains of this neighborhood were fresh, presenting stark testimony to the devastation caused by the rioters. Burnt-out husks of cars littered the streets. Most of the houses were blackened piles of debris, and the ones still intact showed signs of siege: broken windows, singed walls, damaged doors. The acrid odor of charred wood mixed with something indefinable hung in the air despite the freshening effects of the rain.

They walked solemnly up the deserted street, looking for signs of life, but found only ruin. One of the houses, near the end of the second block, had yellow crime scene tape fluttering from the yawning doorway. With a detached sense of horror, Freya assumed it represented loss of human life.

"I've never been out here," she said. "How far is it to the bridge?"

"I don't know, but I think there's a boatyard up ahead. Used to be a huge parking lot for a park or something. There might be someone there who can help us."

She doubted the boatyard was still in business when its neighbors and customers had deserted the area, but she didn't voice her misgivings.

At the end of the last street, Dan took her through an undeveloped section of land where the dark skeletons of trees and bushes testified to a wildfire that had swept through. They crossed a few streets and then entered the boatyard via a wide gap torn in the chain link fence. On the other side, they wandered past aisle after aisle of old boats, from canoe-sized to yacht, most up on cinder blocks or metal stands, but some stacked against each other like dominoes. None of the boats looked seaworthy; the place was clearly a maritime graveyard as desolate as everything else in this forsaken place.

The wind whistled through sailboat rigging and the rain drummed upon hollow surfaces. To make matters worse, it was getting dark, and it was highly unlikely that city services like streetlights were working here.

They rounded a corner and saw an orange glow up ahead some distance. It appeared to be a fire burning in a garbage can, something that would only be possible in this rain if whatever was burning had been doused with a flammable chemical. Whoever set the fire was doubtless someone they should avoid.

She exchanged a glance with Dan, and in unspoken agreement, they turned around and started back the way they'd come.

"We can circle around to the main road," he said quietly.

Suddenly, off to their right behind a stack of wooden pallets, a man's voice called, "Where you been?"

Freya and Dan stopped walking and looked at each other uneasily.

Another voice, also male, responded, "Pac heard something out at Edgemere, so we checked it out."

"See anything?"

"Nah, but someone was there. Rain washed away the tracks, but I found this here umbrella."

"Why, that's a mighty fine parasol," the first man said with phlegmy laugh. "It suits you."

"Does it make me look pretty?"

More laughter, this time from multiple sources, and she could tell they were coming closer.

Dan pushed her ahead of him into a shadowed gap between two boats. They stood facing each other, so close in the narrow space that she felt the warmth of his breath on her temple. Within moments, four roughly dressed men strode past, casually discussing the intruders at Edgemere and its possible meaning. The man holding Freya's umbrella was looking up into its underside as he spun it between his hands.

After their voices faded away, Dan cautiously peeked around the corner. "They're gone."

"Let's get out of here," she said.

They walked fast after that, occasionally breaking into a jog. Moments after they reached the chain link fence and ducked through the opening, someone behind them yelled, "Hey, you!"

Without bothering to look at whoever had called after them, Dan grabbed Freya's hand and they started to run.

Chapter Twelve

They sprinted all the way to down to the main road but slowed to a fast walk when it looked as if no one was chasing them. There were no cars on the road, which ran parallel to the bay maybe a hundred feet to their right. When Dan had been around ten years old, his parents had brought him on a day trip to the other side of the peninsula – the beach side further down from Edgemere. He remembered his dad saying how it was a shame the area hadn't rebounded after Hurricane Poppy. Now the riots seemed to have dealt it the final death blow.

From here, he could see the bridge maybe a mile up ahead. The rain had let up considerably, and he was beginning to think their misadventure was nearly over. Then he spotted a group of six people down the road coming purposefully towards them.

"Ah, shit," he muttered.

Freya clutched his arm. "Where'd they come from?"

"Other side of the boatyard." He glanced in the direction he and Freya had come, and sure enough, another group had appeared. "Classic pinch move."

"What do we do?"

He gestured towards the water. "Can you swim?"

She lifted her soaking wet arms. "Isn't that what we've *been* doing?" Her voice had an hysterical edge to it.

"Maybe they won't hurt us," he said.

She was staring over his shoulder, and the look on her face reminded him of when she'd seen the dog. With a sinking feeling, he turned and saw the white van headed right for them. He was too stunned to even offer up a sarcastic comment. Once again, he grabbed her hand and they took the only path left to them: the one towards the water. They ran through a wide strip of grassy ground, across an overgrown walking path and up to a low metal fence embedded in concrete. On the other side of the fence was a steep slope

49

covered with large rocks down to the water. There was a boat on the water, tied to an iron stake driven into a seam between rocks.

The van pulled over, and the closest group of men approached it, but Dan and Freya didn't wait to see what would happen. They hopped the fence and began traversing the rocks, slick from the rain. Freya seemed surefooted enough, but he stayed close and kept a handheld out towards her in case she slipped.

The battered aluminum boat had two swiveling bucket seats, one in front and one in back, and was littered with rags, garbage, and fishing gear. Dan squatted down and grabbed the side of the boat to hold it steady for Freya to jump aboard, and then he untied the line before hopping in himself. The boat drifted slowly away from the rocks.

Someone shouted, "Hey! Get the hell out of my boat!"

Dan didn't even look up.

The outboard motor was small, ancient and gasoline powered – and he had no idea how to start it.

"Sit down," Freya said, dropping her backpack on the closest seat. "I got this."

He left her to it while he moved a tackle box aside to sit in the other scratched and torn vinyl seat. Freya knelt down, dropped the motor into the water, and fiddled with it. Then she put one hand on top of the motor to brace herself and yanked the pull cord with the other. Miraculously, the little engine started right up, although from the smoke and the irregular sound of it, they were in for a rough ride. After a bit more fiddling, she grasped the steering handle and rotated it so the propeller turned the bow towards the opposite side of the bay. They surged forward at a decent clip, the bow cutting through the chop and spraying them with water.

Over the noise, Dan heard, "Git back here!"

The presumed owner of the boat, an overweight man in a camouflage down parka, gripped the fence impotently, and even in the twilight, Dan could see his face was florid with anger. Standing next to him was the pregnant woman in the white van who'd shown Dan the holo of Freya. She was staring out at the boat while talking to someone on her holophone.

Aside from the scrap metal Dan had scavenged out of abandoned buildings, he hadn't stolen anything since the first grade, when he'd pocketed his best friend's Spiderman eraser, which he'd then sheepishly put back on his friend's desk ten minutes later. Under the circumstances, he didn't think 'stealing' applied to the boat. 'Appropriated under duress' seemed more fitting. He certainly didn't feel guilty about it.

Maybe two minutes after setting out, however, the engine sputtered and stalled. Freya muttered a few choice words under her breath and squeezed a bulb on what Dan assumed was the fuel line. Then she pulled the cord a few more times and the engine started again but failed within seconds. She opened a compartment, lifted a plastic container that was attached to the fuel line, and gently shook it.

"We're out of gas." She stood and kicked at the trash in the bottom of the boat, sodden from the rain. "With no oars."

They weren't so far from shore that they couldn't hear the owner of the boat shouting, "HA! Serves you right!"

Dan and Freya looked at each other in consternation. He wasn't sure whether to be relieved that they'd gotten away or frightened that they hadn't gotten far enough.

"Well," he said. "The good news is the bad guys are on shore. The bad news is we're adrift at sea and darkness is falling. Does that about sum things up?"

Freya sighed heavily, lifting her backpack and sitting in the other seat. "You left out several key details, like lack of food and water, no holophone, and the distinct possibility that it's going to rain again."

Now that she mentioned it, he *was* hungry. "Got any more protein bars?"

"I wish."

He looked across the water at the lights on far side of the bay, trying to gauge the distance. He could swim well enough, but doubted he'd make it that far – and with no idea how strong the currents were, he wouldn't risk it anyway. There was a much better chance of swimming back to the shore they'd just departed, but it looked like the boatyard squatters were hanging around just in case they tried.

"Alrighty, then." He frowned down at the garbage cluttering the boat. "How 'bout we make ourselves at home?"

Freya pinched a filthy rag between two fingers, made a disgusted face at it, and dropped it into the water. "We should see if we can find anything helpful, like a flare gun. It's the law that every boat has to have one."

"Yeah but be careful. There's hooks all over the place."

They used the last of the light to sort through the boat's contents, the vast majority of which they tossed overboard. Normally, he wouldn't dream of littering, but by unspoken agreement they only tossed the biodegradable stuff. They crushed the cans and plastic bottles and shoved them into the compartment next to the gas container. Hooks and sinkers and stray bits of fishing line went into the tackle box. Dan used one of the rags to mop up the filthy water sloshing around the bottom of the boat, wringing it out over the side repeatedly. There was nothing on board that could be used as an oar, and they didn't find a flare gun or an emergency air horn. Other than a wadded-up plastic tarp that reeked of fish, nothing presented itself as particularly useful. But at least without the clutter there was more legroom.

Freya hadn't complained, but now that they were no longer exerting themselves, she'd begun shivering again. She unzipped her backpack and removed something, then took off her coat, laying it behind her near the motor. With one swift movement, she pulled her shirt off over her head. Darkness had almost fully fallen, but the city lights were reflected by the clouds, and Dan's eyes had adjusted to the resulting ambience enough to see the almost luminescent gleam of her skin. His ran his gaze over her neck and shoulders, skipped over the strip of black fabric covering her chest, and dropped to her abdomen. A gust of wind blew her unique scent his way, and he felt that strange hunger rise up like a wave that threatened to crash over him. Swallowing convulsively, he dropped his head in his hands, a strangled little sound escaping from his throat.

"You okay?" she asked. "You're not seasick, are you?"

He pulled his hands away, glad to see she'd changed into something bulky and dark. "I'm fine."

"Well, I've got some dry clothes here. Um, hold on," with no warning, she removed whatever it was she'd just donned, and handed it to him. "This is probably the only thing that'll fit you."

Dan averted his eyes, but the scent coming off the garment – from the feel of the material, it was a sweatshirt – dragged him briefly back into the rising tide of his hunger. While she rummaged around in her backpack for something else to wear, he concentrated on stripping off his hoodie and t-shirt. The sweatshirt was a tight fit, but it was a relief to get out of his wet things.

"Don't suppose you've got sweat*pants* in there?" He was glad his voice sounded normal.

"Nope." Her words were muffled by whatever she was pulling over her head. When the pale oval of her face reappeared, she said, "But I've got my favorite pajama bottoms. They're stretchy and fuzzy."

He laughed. "Can't believe I'm saying this, but…hand 'em over."

She gave them to him along with a small bundle that turned out to be a pair of socks.

He toed off his shoes and peeled his soaked socks and jeans off, doing his level best not to glance her way as she changed her pants. He thought about leaving his boxers on, but the prospect of chafing urged him to throw modesty to the wind. It's not like she could see much. The pajama

52

bottoms were indeed stretchy, but on him, they were snug, and it took some finagling to shimmy them up over his hairy legs and the clammy skin of his backside.

Once they'd finished dressing, he knelt in the bottom of the boat and leaned over the side to dunk the stinking tarp into the water. He rinsed it as best he could, and then shook it out. "If it starts raining again, we can put this over us."

"Good idea."

He sat back down. With nothing more to do but wait, his senses went on high alert: the chop slapping against the hull and gently rocking the boat, the light breeze cutting through his clothing and soughing in his ears, the lights on the far side of the bay, which seemed to sparkle. Under any other circumstances, he would have found it all invigorating.

"So what now?" he said.

Chapter Thirteen

"I don't know," Freya replied. "People take their boats out at night, right? Maybe someone will find us."

"Or the current will push us to shore."

"Yeah." She tried to sound positive. "I mean, what are the odds we'll float out into open sea?"

"Dunno, but I don't really want to think about that."

"You're right. We should talk about something else."

"How about you tell me why those people were after you? The real reason."

She felt a drop on her cheek and used it to redirect the conversation. "Uh, oh. I think it's raining again."

Dan made a 'humph' sound, but she heard the rustle of the plastic tarp. "It's not big enough to cover the whole boat. Our best bet is to hunker down in the space between the seats."

She cringed at the phrase "hunker down," but he was right. The drop she'd felt wasn't a fluke; the rain had begun to fall more steadily, completely dashing her hopes that it had stopped for the duration. Assuming they were stuck out here all night, they would have to get as comfortable as possible. Sleep, she suspected, would be impossible.

"The seats probably come apart," she said. "We can use them as cushions."

While he dismantled the seats, she felt around inside her backpack. "I've got one pair of jeans and the pajama top left. We can put them over us. Not much of a blanket, but better than nothing."

"I tend to run hot, so you take them."

There wasn't the slightest bit of suggestiveness in his tone, but she felt a blush rise in her cheeks and was glad he couldn't see it. The embarrassment was accompanied by a flare-up of the anxiety she'd been feeling in his presence. Maybe being forced into close confinement would help her get over her unreasonable fear of him…but she doubted it.

After Dan wedged the cushions into the boat's centermost area, they positioned themselves awkwardly in the cramped space. When they finally got situated, they were lying on their backs, shoulders and hips touching, bent knees serving as tent poles for the tarp.

"Comfy?" he asked.

"The Taj Mahal it ain't," she responded drily.

She felt him shrug. "Could be worse."

She thought of and discarded several lame quips. To distract herself from her nervousness, she said, "How did you know about the umbrella trick? To stop the dog."

"Was it a trick?"

"Yeah, it's one of the things you're advised to do."

"Oh. Didn't know that. I guess I just…acted instinctively."

"Well, you've got good instincts."

"Whoa. Was that a compliment?"

"Maybe."

"Because I gotta tell ya, my instincts around you have been pretty messed up."

She hesitated, but then asked, "What do you mean?"

"I don't know. Like I said before, there's something about you."

"I'm not different from any other…" she trailed off.

"Any other what?"

She debated whether to tell him the truth, but finally admitted, "I *am* different."

"How?"

"It's the reason they're after me." She pressed her lips together and sighed out her nose. "You know, I never meant to put you or anyone else in danger."

"I eat danger for breakfast."

"Is that right," she said, relieved that her moment of honesty had passed before she'd blurted out any crucial details. "Toasted and buttered?"

"Of course," he replied, "and don't think I didn't notice the way you avoided answering me. What's different about you?"

Once again, she paused before responding, and he said, "Do you always have to stop and think about what you're going to say? Because it makes it seem like you're lying."

She produced a little squeak of outrage even though his comment wasn't that far off the mark. "Maybe it's because the things you're asking could get you hurt."

"Bit late for that. Just tell me already."

"Fine. I have a xenograft."

He let out a surprised laugh. "That is quite possibly the *last* thing I expected you to say. Where is it? *What* is it?"

"It's on my lower back. An East African naked mole rat."

"A *what*?" His laugh this time was incredulous. "Wow. Okay. Not your average graft. So why are they after you? Was it like the king of all naked mole rats?"

"Something like that."

"There you go being all evasive again."

She twitched her shoulders in irritation. "Well, what's your graft?"

"Just your garden variety snake."

In the blackness under the tarp, she narrowed her eyes. "What kind of snake?"

"Good question. I have no idea."

"How could you not know?"

It was his turn to hesitate, and she pounced. "Ha! You're totally doing what you just accused me of. Have I asked the great Inquisitor a question he doesn't want to answer?"

"No. It's just complicated."

"Welcome to my world."

They fell silent for maybe ten seconds, and then they both spoke at once.

"There was this–" he said.

"I was part of a–" she said.

They laughed, and he said, "You go."

She started talking, haltingly at first, but before she knew it, she was pouring her heart out. She told him about the anguish of losing her father at age forty to colon cancer. The despair of discovering that she'd inherited the genes that caused it. The hope that the xenograft she'd been given by the bioengineers at Falconot Biomedical would imbue her with the graft donor's natural cancer-fighting mechanisms. The miserable weeks not long after the National Library of Medicine had been hacked and the clinical trial's research released to the public, where not a day went by that someone involved in the trial didn't die in a tragic "accident." The days leading up to the inescapable conclusion that she and her mother were next, followed by months of hiding, living in a constant state of paranoia. The only thing she left out was Ryan's status as an XIA agent.

Unloading it all on Dan was nothing short of cathartic, but Freya felt almost foolish after her words trickled to a stop.

"Damn," he said quietly. "That's some story."

"It's the truth."

"I believe you."

The seat cushion dipped as he shifted his weight, and she felt his fingers against her forearm. He slid them along her wrist, presumably fumbling for her hand. She jerked her arm away, a stuttering sound of refusal coming from her throat.

The tarp rustled as he retreated. "Sorry. I forgot you find me repugnant."

"No, I don't. Why do you say that?"

"It's kinda obvious."

"It's just…I'm scared of you for some reason."

"Huh. I scare you, and you make me…"

"What? Exactly how *do* I make you feel?"

Chapter Fourteen

She'd been honest with him, but Dan felt he couldn't return the courtesy – not without driving her further away. She was already afraid of him; what would she do if he told her he'd developed an unnatural appetite for her that even now he fought against succumbing to? She'd probably jump overboard.

His answer took too long, but she didn't accuse him of stonewalling this time. She just waited as he sorted through his thoughts. He decided on a partial truth.

"I don't really know how to put it into words without sounding...insane."

He wished he could see her face, especially as the seconds ticked by with no reply. Finally, she said, "Okay."

It was a cautious response that he interpreted as mistrust, so in an effort to put her at ease, he rambled on. "I mean, I'm not, obviously, insane, but it's like, I get these weird kind of ideas when I'm around you. Which—which sounds bad, but, uh, you're—*you* seem really nice, and—and, um, of course, you know, totally hot and all..."

He clamped his jaw shut several humiliating words too late. In the darkness under the tarp, his gaze darted around as if looking for an invisible escape route.

"Uh...thanks?" she said.

He took a deep breath of fish-scented air, and then sighed long and heavily. "Now you think I'm a complete idiot."

"No. I think you're nice, too."

He winced. Her tone was perfectly pleasant, and he'd called her nice first, but something about the word coming out of *her* mouth sounded like a death knell. Especially since she didn't remark upon his spastic "totally hot" comment. Never in his eighteen years had he butchered an attempted flirtation, if that's what it was, quite so epically. Part of him desperately wanted to fix things, but he'd burned himself so badly he was afraid to say anything else.

"What kind of ideas?" she asked.

He hadn't realized how tense he'd become until his shoulders sagged to the cushions in defeat. "You smell good. Like food."

"Seriously?" he could hear the laughter in her voice.

"Can't make that kind of crazy up."

"Well, you could, but why would you want to?"

Her amusement was patently obvious, and catchy. He smiled in the dark. "I don't know. Sheer entertainment value?"

"So, am I in danger of getting nommed on?"

He sucked air through his teeth in a sibilant slurp. "Maybe."

"Okay, now I can't tell if you're serious or not."

He rolled partially towards her, expecting her to protest when his knee came to rest against hers, but she didn't. "What kind of perfume do you wear?"

"I don't."

"Shampoo?"

"Um, whatever Carla uses. Something generic."

"Who's Carla? Oh, wait. You mean Mouse?"

"Yeah," she said.

"Alright. I just saw her a few days ago and she smells like cigarettes, so that's not it. What about lotion? Or laundry soap?"

"Negative on the lotion, and my mom uses whatever's on sale to wash clothes."

He pulled the neckline of the sweatshirt she'd given him up and over his nose and inhaled. The faint scent lingering in the fabric smelled pretty much the same as his own clothes, except for something…else. But she'd worn it briefly before taking it off and giving it to him. "I don't think it's the laundry soap. Honestly? I think it's your skin. Maybe if I…"

"What? Sniff me?" She snorted in laughter.

"That was ladylike."

She elbowed him in the side. "I'm not the one going around sniffing people."

"I realize it would be hard for me to sound any creepier."

"Ya think?"

A flurry of raindrops pelted the tarp, and the boat rocked. He heard her shaky indrawn breath and tried to think of something reassuring to say. Before he could spout something invariably inane, she twisted towards him and socked him accidentally in the nose.

"Ow!" he exclaimed, even though it didn't really hurt.

59

"Sorry!" she said, laughing again. "I was just—if you want to smell my wrist…"

He found her hand and pulled it towards his face, pressing her wrist against the space between his lips and nose. He braced himself for a resurgence of that nearly overwhelming urge to *attack*, but nothing happened. The urge was still there in the background but smelling her wrist didn't exacerbate the problem. If anything, he had to fight the impulse to kiss her velvety skin.

"Well," he said, releasing her hand, "that's a big negative."

"So you can't smell it at all now?"

"I smell fish."

"Which lets me off the hook, no pun intended, as a potential snack?"

He considered it. "Maybe it's not coming from your wrist."

After a moment, she said, "You think it's my xenograft?"

"Makes sense, doesn't it?"

"Not really."

"I'm a snake and you're a rat." As the answer hit home, he felt a tremendous sense of relief. "You're my *prey*."

Chapter Fifteen

"That's why I asked what kind of snake your donor was," she said. "I researched naked mole rats, and there's a particular East African snake that goes after them. You didn't react to Carla, and she has a mouse graft."

"What kind of snake was it?"

She shrugged. "Can't remember, but even if I could, how would you know?"

"I wouldn't, but now I'm thinking I probably should. I mean, I've heard stories about how grafts can have an effect on their hosts."

"Like curing cancer?" she asked.

"No, like…take Wade's dad for instance. You ever heard of the Clan?"

"It's a xeno gang, right?"

"Yeah. They all have spotted hyena grafts. Wade's dad is a member. His xeno name is Cerberus, like the hellhound."

She shuddered.

"Wade says the graft changed him. Made him, I don't know, more aggressive, but at the same time completely subservient to the leader of the gang."

"Wow. What's Wade's graft?"

"A skunk."

"Ew."

"Well, he doesn't *stink*."

"I beg to differ."

"Ha ha. I mean he didn't have the scent glands grafted on, just the skin."

"I know what you meant," she said. "Did his graft change him?"

"Not that I noticed. People have always avoided him."

"What about you? Other than the weirdness with me, anything different?"

"Nope."

The boat suddenly rocked from side to side, throwing Freya against Dan and back again. She'd been out on Perch Pond in her Grandpa Pat's boat dozens of times, which is how she'd known how to start the outboard motor. However, she'd never been on the water at night, nor on the ocean in such rough conditions. Not to mention being trapped under a foul-smelling tarp with guy who was convinced he was her predator. She was having a hard time keeping her fear at bay.

The boat rocked again, and then once more, in a familiar pattern.

"That's a boat wake!" She bolted upright, slapping the tarp aside.

They'd drifted closer to the bridge, and to the left of them she saw the running lights of a much larger vessel. She half-stood, waving her arms even though the other boat's occupants wouldn't be able to see her in the dark.

"Hey!" she yelled. "*Over here!*"

Dan joined her, and together they shouted, but the boat slid silently past.

"Noooo," she cried, slumping down onto the cushions.

"Wait," Dan said. "Look!"

She lifted her head and saw that the other boat had slowed. Someone on deck switched on a bright light and directed it at the water. She and Dan began yelling again. The beam swung their way and stopped when it reached them. She grinned like a fool, spontaneously throwing her arms around Dan, but letting go almost as quickly.

After about five minutes, she heard the purr of a well-tuned outboard engine, which got louder until an inflatable boat entered the circle of the spotlight. Its pilot pulled up alongside their boat, bumping the side gently. Dan knelt and reached out for it, but suddenly recoiled and turned to Freya.

"It's them," he said grimly.

She gasped and looked at the man in the inflatable. The light from behind put him in silhouette and highlighted the multitude of raindrops, making it impossible to see his face, but she recognized his bulky outline. It was the big man from the white van.

"Don't give me no trouble," the man said. "We ain't gonna hurt ya. Queen just wants to talk. Now git on board."

Freya glanced behind her at the black water, trying to muster the courage to dive overboard, but the man said, "Current under that bridge is wicked fast, and you don't look like no fish to me."

Still she hesitated, weighing her only options: jump overboard, or surrender to the people she'd been running from. Which option would kill her faster? The man said they only wanted to talk, but the car chase suggested otherwise. Yet assuming his warning regarding the current was true, why hadn't he just let her dive in? As far as arranging an accidental death went, that would have been the easiest path for him to take.

"Listen." The man's deep voice softened. "This is just an exchange of information, I swear. Plus, you look like you could use a bit of rescuing." He held out a hand.

Freya had been caught between a rock and a hard place before, but never when her life was on the line. Her instincts told her this man was dangerous, but his voice, mannerisms, and gesture – hand out, palm up – seemed nonthreatening. She'd assumed he and his companion were involved with whomever wanted her dead, but what if that wasn't the case? She took a deep breath, a huge chance, and grasped his hand. While the man helped her into the inflatable, Dan gathered up their belongings.

The short trip to what turned out to be a luxury yacht was uneventful. Once they got on board, the man led them up a flight of stairs and inside a surprisingly large salon, where the warmth was the only thing Freya welcomed. There, the pregnant woman from the van was waiting with an older woman, tall, with white-blond hair that hung to her low back. There was something wrong with one of her eyes; the iris was reddish tinted, reflecting the light like a cat's eyes.

She swept her gaze over them, haughty and calculating, and yet her words were spoken with amusement. "You led my people a merry chase."

"Who are you?" Freya asked.

"My name is Maddy. This is Padme and that's Oscar," she gestured towards the big man. "I know *you* are Freya Jones, a.k.a. Amanda Sullivan." She looked from Freya to Dan. "And your protector…?"

For a disconcerting moment, Freya thought she'd said "predator." While she was gathering her wits, Dan said, "She's perfectly capable of protecting herself."

The corners of Maddy's red lips turned up slightly. "I don't doubt it. Your name?"

"Dan."

"Well then. Dan. Freya. Welcome aboard the Phoenix." She eyed Dan's attire and the bundle of clothing he held. "Oscar, would you please see to it that our guests' things are washed and dried?"

Oscar nodded, took the bundle from Dan and left the salon.

"May I offer you a drink, or perhaps something to eat?" Maddy said.

"Is it going to be our last meal?" Freya asked.

Maddy chuckled. "I have no intention of harming you. In fact, having searched for you for some weeks now, I'm in the mood for a

63

celebration. We have pizza and soda…" she said the last bit with an enticing lilt in her voice.

Freya was starving and the thought of pizza made her stomach growl, but she said, "No, thank you. I just want to go home."

Maddy made a "tch" sound. "I'm afraid that would be inadvisable. We only found you because we've been monitoring communications between my father's soldiers. We beat them to you, but only by minutes. Oscar saw their car and called in an anonymous tip to the police, but by now they surely know where you were staying."

"Your father's *soldiers*?" Freya shook her head in confusion.

"Employees. And no, I don't suppose you have any idea who is behind what's happened to you," Maddy said. "I wouldn't have known anything about the whole sordid mess myself, except Oscar used to be one of my father's underpaid and underappreciated personal guards, which is how we found out about some of the more frightful things dear old Dad's been up to."

"Who is he?" Dan asked. "Your father."

"Philip Singh, billionaire, corrupt to the very bottom of his blackened soul."

"Singh?" Freya said.

Through Ryan, she knew Philip Singh had been involved in the plot to blow up Poppy's Pier, but his attorneys and an army of publicists had managed to make him look like a victim in the public eye. Ryan had told her mother that Singh owned a major news corporation, so it wasn't difficult for his people to warp the truth through liberal use of that resource. It was painfully ironic that Singh was suing the XIA – and Ryan and his fellow agents specifically – for doing their job protecting the public but failing to obtain solid evidence against him.

"Oh, you've heard of him," Maddy said with a sardonic lift of one brow.

Freya nodded, but cautiously. She also knew that Maddy Singh had been head of the xenofreak Mad Eye gang. For Ryan's safety as an undercover agent, it was imperative Freya not reveal that she knew more about Maddy's and Philip Singh's activities than the average person. "Would it be possible for me to call my mom?" she asked instead.

Maddy lifted her chin, regarding Freya through narrowed eyes. "I truly wish you could. I imagine she's worried sick, but by now her phone will have been jacked, and she'll have multiple tails wherever she goes. Frankly, both you and your mother are safer if she doesn't know where you are. Once you make contact, my father's men will most certainly take her to use as leverage."

"*Take* her?" Freya's voice was hardly above a whisper. She told herself that Ryan would get to her mom before Singh's soldiers, but telling herself and convincing herself were too different things entirely.

Maddy tutted, strode over to a table, and opened a pizza box. "My dear girl. You really must eat something. Getting through this sort of thing requires sustenance!"

Freya walked towards the table on leaden feet. She didn't trust Maddy, but in her heart, she knew she was right.

Chapter Sixteen

Dan had never seen the leader of the Mad Eye, but he'd heard enough about her to recognize her on sight, especially given that Oscar had said, "Queen only wants to talk." Maddy hadn't mentioned the Mad Eye to Freya, but she'd verified her identity to Dan as soon as she'd said her father's name. Purportedly, Maddy Singh had some quirky personality traits; most notably, she'd taken on the guise of "benevolent ruler" to the members of her gang – adopting the role of Mad Eye Queen, a doubly ironic turn of phrase given that she was transgender, and one of her eyes was red. He'd heard that her xenograft was a pig eye, done in an attempt to replace the albino eyes she was born with, but establishing vision in the transplant had failed.

The pepperoni pizza was cold, but Dan scarfed down two slices before Freya had nibbled her way to the crust on her first. Maddy left the salon to go talk to the captain, leaving the young woman named Padme to watch over them.

"Would it be possible for me to call *my* mom?" he asked her.

She had been standing near the door but walked over to where Dan and Freya sat at the table. "You don't fully understand the gravity of your situation, do you?"

"I guess not. Why don't you spell it out for us?"

Padme lifted a hand to her head, and at first, he thought she was going to tuck her dark brown hair behind her ear, but instead she took what he thought at first was a lock of it between her fingers and rubbed. A second look confirmed that she was caressing the tip of one of her xenografts, which appeared to be the upside-down ears of a cow.

"If Philip Singh finds you, he will kill you. Nothing you can do or say will prevent it," Padme said.

"If he's so dangerous, why is Maddy helping us?" he asked.

"There's bad blood between them. He's hurt her in unimaginable ways, as only family can."

"Not my family."

"Mine either," Freya said.

Padme's smile didn't reach her eyes. "Lucky you."

Dan heard a subtle change in the yacht's engine and almost lost his balance as the vessel accelerated into a turn. "Where are we going?"

Padme shrugged. "Somewhere safer than here."

Maddy sashayed back into the salon and put her hands on her hips. "I can't tell you how pleased I am that I found you."

Dan knew she was addressing Freya even though she looked at both of them.

"How long are you going to keep us?" Freya asked.

"Well, that depends upon a lot of things, several of which I have little control over. Now that you've eaten, tell me, why exactly *does* my father want you dead?"

Freya's eyebrows lifted in surprise. "You don't know?"

Maddy shook her head. "Oscar wasn't privy to everything my father did, but if he happened to be in the room when he was conducting business, he tried to pay attention – strictly for self-preservation, mind you, considering how expendable my father considered his underlings. What I *know* is that my father desperately wants you found and disposed of."

"Oh," Freya said faintly. "Well…I'm not sure why he's after us, really. I mean, it has something to do with my graft, obviously–"

"You're a xeno?" It was Padme.

Freya nodded. "I was part of a research study."

Maddy's mouth dropped open, but then she closed it with an audible click of her teeth, the muscles in her jaw clenching. "Go on."

Freya folded her hands together on the table and launched into the same story she'd told Dan but added the additional details of the day's events. Maddy interrupted a few times to clarify things, but otherwise listened avidly. When Freya finished speaking, a small silence fell. Then Maddy turned to Dan.

"So you and Freya just met three days ago?"

"Pretty much," he said.

"But you knew all about this?" She waved a hand in Freya's general direction.

"No. She just told me a little while ago. On the fishing boat."

Maddy crossed her arms and jutted her jaw to one side. "She's a virtual stranger, yet you took a big risk aiding her escape."

He wasn't sure what she was getting at but responded honestly. "I didn't know at the time how big a risk it was going to be."

"I see."

"You know, my mom's going to call the police when I don't come home, and my friends are going to tell them what happened."

"Undoubtedly, and since my father has eyes and ears everywhere, that information will eventually reach him. He will send his people after you, and we will be waiting."

Dan stared at her in disbelief. "You're using us as bait."

"Technically, I'm using *her* as bait." Maddy nodded in Freya's direction. "To draw my father out."

"Why?" Freya asked.

"If you must know, he tried to kill me – as well as every xeno who was rounded up during the riots and sent to Poppy's Pier. I'd rather like to return the favor."

"So it's true," Freya said. "What they say about him."

"That he's a monster?" Maddy shrugged. "Yes."

"No, that he was involved with what happened at the pier."

Maddy suddenly looked bored with the conversation. "If it's illegal, immoral, or even marginally profitable to his corporation? He's involved."

Oscar came back into the salon, and Maddy said, "It's getting late. Oscar will show you to your cabin."

Dan still had at least a dozen questions, but the Mad Eye queen no longer seemed amenable to them.

"Uh, cabin?" Freya asked, glancing at Dan. "As in...*one* cabin?"

"I do have a crew," Maddy replied. "Accommodations are at a premium, but the cabin has bunk beds, so you needn't worry about propriety."

Oscar stood aside and lifted a hand to indicate they should precede him out the door. Freya looked like she wanted to protest, but then her expression changed to one of resignation. She went through the doorway, and Dan followed her down a corridor.

"Bathroom's on this side," Oscar said, placing a hand on a door to his right. "Your cabin's there." He pointed to a door on his left. "Don't want to have to lock you in, so no wandering around, hear?"

Dan and Freya nodded. They entered the narrow space and Oscar said, "Good night," before shutting the door.

Dan surveyed their accommodations. There wasn't a porthole, but a crystal light fixture in the ceiling cast a dim glow over the subdued opulence. The shiny white plastic walls and warm wooden accents couldn't disguise how small the cabin was. The bunk beds were slightly wider than a surfboard, and when he sat on the lower mattress, about as comfortable. There were built in cupboards facing the bunk; he reached out and opened one, it had linens inside.

"You want the top or bottom?" he asked.

Freya made a little choking sound, and he looked over at her. She'd placed both hands over her face and was bent nearly double. It took a moment for him to realize she was silently sobbing.

Appalled, Dan abruptly stood, completely forgetting the upper bunk. His head hit the frame with a solid *thunk*, and he collapsed back onto the mattress. Out of respect for Freya's state of mind, he didn't cry out, but the pain made his eyes water. As soon as it faded enough for him to regain control of his faculties, he stood more carefully, and then gently put his arm around her shoulders. He halfway expected her to push him away, but instead she turned to him. He wrapped her in a comforting embrace, and she buried her face in the crook of his neck while he murmured soothing words of solace and patted her on the back.

It took about ten minutes for her to get it all out. When she lifted her head and moved away from him, Dan was astonished that her swollen eyes and red nose didn't detract from her beauty. He hooked a finger under the neck of his borrowed sweatshirt and pulled the soaked fabric away from his skin.

"I need to use the restroom," she said, avoiding eye contact.

When the door closed behind her, he realized he hadn't felt the urge to bite her the entire time.

Chapter Seventeen

When Freya reentered the "cabin" that was more like a closet, Dan was lying on his side under the blanket on the top bunk, elbow bent, head resting in his hand. He'd taken her sweatshirt off and hung it on a hook on the back of the door.

"You okay?" he asked.

"Fine," she replied.

"Bottom bunk alright?"

"Yeah."

"Well…goodnight then."

"'Night."

She switched off the light and sat on the thin mattress for a few minutes, mind drifting aimlessly through the events of the day. She felt numb, which was better than before, when she'd lost control and bawled like a baby. She wasn't embarrassed exactly but wished the sob-fest hadn't happened. Dan probably thought she was weak as a day-old kitten. Not that she cared…but then as soon as the thought occurred to her she realized she *did* care. He'd told Maddy Singh that she didn't need protecting, but now she was afraid her blubbering outburst may have changed his opinion.

She lay down and made herself as comfortable as possible in this strange place under even stranger circumstances. She was afraid the movement of the yacht would make her seasick, but instead the rocking motion lulled her to sleep.

Thumping sounds woke her sometime later. She raised up on her elbows in the darkness, calling out, "Who's there?"

"It's just me." Dan's sheepish voice came not from the upper bunk, but from the floor.

"What happened?" she asked.

"Fell out of bed," he said.

"Are you hurt?"

"Nah, but the storm's gotten worse."

The yacht was no longer merely rocking; it was pitching slowly up and slowly down like it was navigating large swells. Freya felt herself slide a few inches across the mattress with each one. Over the steady background hum of the engine, she heard the occasional groan of protest from the yacht's infrastructure.

"I'm turning on the light," he said.

She put a hand over her eyes, and once the light was on, saw from under her fingers that he was standing right in front of her. She got a good look at his shirtless abdomen and chest as he pulled the mattress from the top bunk with the harsh ripping sound of Velcro releasing.

"I'm gonna sleep on the floor," he said. "Don't, uh, step on me if you have to get up."

"Could you leave the light on? I mean, just in case something bad happens."

"Yeah, okay."

He lay on the mattress and wriggled around for a few minutes, clearly trying to get comfortable, before finally settling down.

As tired as she was, she couldn't fall back asleep, and the rough sea didn't help matters. All she could think was how frantic with worry her mother must be. After lying awake with her mind spinning for what felt like an hour, she opened her eyes and looked at Dan, hoping to distract herself. He had turned away from her, so she was free to study what she could see of him. The rain had obliterated whatever attempts he'd made this morning to style his hair, and his overgrown brown locks curled riotously against his pillow and the nape of his neck. The blanket was tucked under his arm, and the light accentuated the muscles in his shoulder and upper back.

On the fishing boat, lying next to him under the tarp, she'd been nervous, and not just because of her insistent fear of him. She was seventeen years old, and other than a two week "relationship" in the eighth grade, and a few stolen kisses at summer camp, she'd never had a boyfriend. She'd spent all of her free time with her father during his illness, and then after he passed, grief had filled every waking moment for months on end. Her crushes had all been for celebrities, which left her with very little experience that wasn't pure fantasy.

Dan, however, was a real live boy who'd called her "totally hot." He'd gone to great lengths to help her, so she was pretty sure he liked her. As for how she felt about him, the whole predator-prey thing had put a damper on things up to this point. It occurred to her that since her days might very well be numbered, being in close quarters with him could be considered an opportunity.

71

Dan's breathing was steady, and she noticed the minuscule movement of the pulse in his neck. As if he sensed her regard, he rolled over suddenly, and she met his heavy-lidded gaze before looking away.

"Can't sleep?" he said.

She didn't trust her voice, so she shook her head.

"You're not sick, are you?"

"I'm fine. It's just…"

"Been a long, crazy day."

She sighed. "Yeah."

"We're gonna be all right," he said.

"How do you know?"

"I just do."

"Do you trust her? Maddy."

"Hell, no. Do you know who she is?"

She nodded.

"Oh, that's right. Your cousin. Was he a Mad Eye?"

"Not that I know of. What did Ryan – I mean Knuckles – do to Wade's dad?"

"Grease fight, before the riots. Broke his arm. Cerberus isn't in the hospital anymore, though. Wade just said that to mess with him."

By now, Ryan would have found Wade and gotten him to talk. Ryan would know the last place Freya had been seen alive was Edgemere, but that didn't mean he'd be able to convince his boss to allocate XIA resources to search for her. Knowing Ryan, he'd look for her anyway. She had no idea whether any of the Edgemere locals that had chased them knew that she and Dan were now on Maddy's yacht, but she hoped so, and hoped Ryan would get it out of them. She wondered if Maddy's involvement would prompt the director of the XIA to finally open an investigation, especially considering that Freya's whereabouts, according to Maddy, would definitely find its way to Philip Singh.

Dan sat up and crossed his arms over his chest. "There's something I keep meaning to tell you about my graft."

She shifted onto her side, noticing that the light brought out little highlights on the scales wrapped around his upper arm. Impulsively, she reached out and gently grasped his arm below the graft. She ran her thumb across the scales. "Feels dry. Does it shed?"

"Yeah, just did a few weeks ago."

"You wanna see mine?" He was the first person she'd ever told, and the first person she *wanted* to show her graft to.

He looked surprised, but then grinned. "Alright."

72

Now that she'd made the offer, a flare of nervous energy surged through her. Before she could weasel out of it, she pushed her blanket down and rolled onto her stomach. Just before she lifted her sweater, she remembered to turn her head to watch his reaction.

He didn't just look, however. He got up onto his knees and placed a hand on the mattress on the far side of her hip to support his upper body as he leaned over her. With a fascinated look on his face, he lowered his head to within a few inches of her lower back. His warm breath sent shivers up and down her spine.

"That's it," he said. "That's the scent that makes me want to…"

He pushed abruptly away from her bunk and she caught a wild look in his eyes before he turned his back on her.

"You alright?" She reached out for his shoulder, but as soon as she touched him, he said in a subdued voice, "Don't."

She yanked her sweater down and retreated under her blanket, trying not to let the rejection hurt; telling herself he was simply trying to regain control of himself. After a moment, he got to his feet and headed for the cabin door, muttering something about the bathroom.

She closed her eyes, reproachfully thinking that even though he'd told her he'd been struggling with his strange urges, she'd just had to poke that bear. She should have realized how it would affect him but had been too focused on her own mixed feelings.

She curled up in the fetal position, listening for him. No doubt he'd come back in and act like nothing had happened, like the connection between them wasn't messing with his head. She wondered if they would have even met if that connection didn't exist. He might not have noticed her at all without his graft's influence over him. The fact that that influence was manufactured only increased her resentment of it.

Chapter Eighteen

Dan cupped his hands under the cold running water and splashed it on his face, then looked into the mirror over the sink. The fluorescent light in the tiny bathroom made his face look haggard, or maybe that was just backlash from his reaction to Freya's graft.

It had taken all his willpower to walk away from her. His insight on the fishing boat, that he was a predator and she his prey, had just been confirmed, and then some. To make matters worse, the compulsion to attack her was tightly intertwined with his attraction for her, and he honestly didn't know what he was capable of. Never in his life had he so thoroughly doubted his own intentions.

He glanced down at a pile of clothing on the floor near the toilet. Oscar must have put their clothes on the closed toilet lid for them to find, but the rough sea had dislodged them. He took his time changing back into his jeans, t-shirt and hoodie, hoping the longer he stalled, the more control over his unnatural appetite he'd gain. His tennis shoes and Freya's boots had also been cleaned and dried. Oscar must be a full-service kind of thug.

Dan set Freya's clothes on the edge of the little sink and sat on the toilet lid to put his shoes on, even though he wasn't going anywhere. After he'd tied them, he rested his elbows on his knees and his chin in his hands, stalling. He didn't want to go back into the cabin; afraid he'd take one look at her and lose control again.

His stomach growled, and he let out a little laugh. Just the thought of her brought his hunger to the surface. He frowned and stood as something occurred to him.

Oscar had warned them not to wander around the yacht, but Dan took a chance and snuck down the hallway to the salon. A holoclock on the wall read 4:33 a.m. Muted lighting showed him the way to the refrigerator in the compact kitchenette. Inside, he found the leftover box of pizza. He'd eaten two slices earlier, but that hardly satisfied him on a good night, so he helped himself to three more, washing it all down with a soda. Once he was done, he went quietly back to the cabin.

Freya's eyes were closed, but something told him she was awake.

He sat cross-legged on his mattress, watching her face.

Several minutes passed. He thought maybe her eyelids flickered once; perhaps she'd lifted them slightly only to find him staring.

"Freya," he whispered.

She opened her eyes.

"I might have figured something out," he said.

"What?"

"I think maybe my reaction is harder to control when I'm hungry."

"Maybe you should eat something, then."

"I did. Had some more pizza."

She nodded, but he could tell she was still wary of him. Then she said, "What were you going to tell me? About your graft."

"Right. Um…it's for research, too."

"It is?"

"Yeah. I answered an ad and they accepted me. The graft was free, but I had to agree to fill out a questionnaire once a week."

"What are they researching?"

"I don't know."

"You don't know what kind of snake your donor was, and you don't know why they gave you the graft…what *do* you know?"

Dan frowned. She made it sound like he was an idiot, and he was beginning to wonder himself. "I guess not as much as I should. But in my defense, this was right after the riots and it seemed like a good way to protect myself from the super typhoid."

"Depends on who you got your graft from," she said.

"What do you mean?"

She shrugged. "A lot of the newer donors have been bioengineered so they don't protect us anymore."

"How do you know that?"

She looked to the left and the right, like she was worried someone might overhear. "I can't tell you."

He lifted his eyebrows. "Why not?"

"I just can't."

"Okay," he said doubtfully.

"So, who is it that gave you the graft?" she asked.

"A company called Matrixeno."

"Do you know anything about them?"

"Never heard of them before this, and no, I didn't bother researching them. Go ahead, tell me what a moron I am."

She smiled. "They're probably legit. I'm just paranoid."

"With good reason."

She sighed and closed her eyes. "Can we sleep now? I'm wiped."

"Yeah, sure." His intention had been to ask her if he could test his reaction to her graft again, but her request put the kibosh on that.

He lay down, noticing as he adjusted his blanket that the sea had calmed. He wondered if they'd made port somewhere, and it was his last thought before drifting off.

Chapter Nineteen

Freya woke with a start when the door to the cabin banged open. Maddy Singh stood in the doorway, dressed in a white button-down shirt and snug black slacks. Her hair was plaited into two braids. She held a holo tablet in one hand and was tapping the fingers of her other hand against her thigh like she'd already had too much coffee.

"Wakey-wakey," she sang. "There are a few things we need to discuss."

Freya, sleep-deprived after her rough night, rubbed her eyes. Next to her on the floor, Dan stretched and sat up, his curly hair mussed.

Maddy's fingers kept up the rapid tapping as Freya and Dan got groggily to their feet.

"Follow me," Maddy said. "Breakfast is ready."

Freya gestured to the bathroom door. "Um..."

Maddy smiled. "We'll wait."

Inside, Freya found the clothes she'd been wearing the day before, cleaned, dried, and folded. After she used the facilities, she changed into her jeans and shirt, and then shrugged into her wool coat and pulled her boots on. Back out in the corridor, Maddy marched them to the salon, where steaming plates of scrambled eggs, bacon and biscuits awaited them. Freya and Dan sat at the table while Oscar poured orange juice into cut crystal glasses. Padme stood silently to one side, always watchful.

Dan shoved an entire piece of bacon into his mouth and spoke around it. "Where are we?"

"A little farther up the coast," Maddy said. "I need to ask you about your graft."

"Me?" Dan asked, because Maddy was looking at him when she said it.

"Yes, you."

"Okay."

Maddy glanced down at her holo tablet. "You obtained it from Matrixeno, correct?"

"Yeah, how'd you know?"

"Matrixeno is a bioengineering firm owned by a series of shell corporations that I suspect are connected to my father, although he's rather good at hiding assets."

"Really? That's...strange," Dan said, glancing at Freya.

Maddy's lips twisted. "I believe the word you're looking for is 'coincidental,' although I doubt it applies here."

"You didn't answer how you knew where he got his graft," Freya said.

Padme said, "No one promised you privacy."

Freya stared at her. "You bugged our cabin?"

"Not your cabin specifically," Maddy replied. "The entire yacht is under constant surveillance."

While Freya absorbed that little tidbit, Dan asked, "Why do you think it isn't a coincidence?"

Maddy smiled. "Because Padme passed Matrixeno's name along to a very talented colleague on shore who managed to hack into their main server this morning. He found the research study," she made quotation marks with her fingers, "that gave you your graft. The study's stated purpose is to monitor grafted subjects for any detrimental health effects. The unstated point being to emphasize its *negative* impact, which is entirely aligned with my father's thinking."

Dan sighed. "So, Freya was right. It's not legit."

"On the contrary, it seems to be quite above board. Unless you dig a little deeper, which we did."

Freya met Dan's gaze. Neither of them was surprised by Maddy's words.

"Were you aware," Maddy continued, "that all the Matrixeno graftees are high school students over the age of eighteen?"

Dan had just shoved a big bite of eggs into his mouth. He shook his head no.

"According to internal memos," Maddy said, "the study's goal was to maintain one grafted male student per high school throughout the five boroughs. Each of the students was grafted with the skin of a rufous beaked snake and required to fill out a weekly questionnaire."

"Rufous beaked snake," Dan repeated, looking at Freya again.

"It's from East Africa," she said. "Like my graft."

"Lemme guess," he said. "Naked mole rats are its preferred food source."

Freya pressed her lips together and lifted her eyebrows in acknowledgment.

"They knew," he said, shaking his head. "The questionnaire was trying to determine whether I'd met someone with your specific graft." His face fell into a look of horrified realization. "It was me. I'm how they found you."

"Yes," Maddy said, "but technically, they *didn't* find her, so don't beat yourself up about it. Besides, you couldn't possibly have known."

Freya set her fork down and turned to Maddy in consternation. "All that just to find *me*?"

Maddy shrugged. "I presume that in my father's warped perception of things, the stakes were high enough. And keep in mind that your running told him you knew you were in danger, which meant you could potentially expose all those accidental deaths you told me about as murder."

"But *why* did he murder everyone?" Freya's voice broke.

"I'm glad you asked, but first, some backstory. You already know about the National Library of Medicine hack that brought a goodly amount of unpublished xeno research to light. *That* brilliant bit of tomfoolery was accomplished by Padme's aforementioned colleague, at the behest of her former employer, Nicolas Fournier, more commonly known as The Bestia Butcher, leader of the XBestia. I see from your expression that you know about him, and before you deny it, I'll just toss it out there that I'm aware your cousin is XIA. I'll explain *how* I know in a moment."

Freya frowned and looked guiltily at Dan. "I couldn't tell you."

He didn't respond other than to shake his head slightly, a look of bewilderment on his face.

Maddy continued. "If Fournier hadn't hacked the National Library, none of those studies would have ever been released, and if you're asking yourself why not, know that in the medical research world, the peer review system, or quality control if you will, is biased, because, and this is going to tickle you pink, men like my father made sure of it. He has undue influence throughout the American political system, including within agencies like the FDA and CDC, and he's besties with Governor Koontz. Unfortunately for you, the study you were participating in showed real promise, something at odds with my father's goals. When you asked why he went to all the trouble of setting up a real research study to find you, keep in mind it also gave him the opportunity to cast negative aspersions on the practice of xenografting. It seems his burning desire is to debunk anything and everything positively associated with it. And now I suppose you're asking yourself, 'To what end?'"

"Because he sells drugs," Freya said. "Legally, I mean. And if the illnesses his drugs treat are suddenly curable, he's out a lot of money."

"That's correct." Maddy seemed mildly surprised. "I see your cousin has kept you informed."

"You said you'd tell me how you knew about him," Freya said. "Ryan."

"Ryan? Oh, Agent Boardman, of course. Well, he and I encountered each other a few times during the riot, but I didn't know he was your cousin until this morning. Padme's friend managed to get quite a bit of information out of the Matrixeno hack. In fact, I think the easiest thing is to let you read for yourself." She held out her holo tablet, and Freya took it. It was in 2D mode and displayed a wall of text.

She skimmed the first paragraph, an abstract written by the company that had done the research on Freya's graft, Falconot Biomedical. It was heavy on medical terminology describing the purpose of the naked mole rat study. The second paragraph, also penned by Falconot, but dated eighteen months into the study, was filled with even more densely packed medical-speak, but seemed to be saying the study had shown encouraging results thus far. The next section was titled, "Subject Profiles," and the date at the top was a few weeks after the National Library of Medicine hack when the public got access to all that research. The author of this section wasn't identified, but right away it was clear to Freya that Falconot staff hadn't written it.

As she silently read the profiles, she was filled with fascinated revulsion.

"Subject One is a twenty-two-year-old male in good health. Employed as a bartender in Queens. Lives with mother in a house located four blocks from Subject's place of employment. House is secured via exterior cameras. Subject is single and likely heterosexual. Subject completed high school with average grades and has not pursued higher education. Surveillance unit reports Subject's scheduled workdays vary, but the hours are always 8pm to 3am. Subject often appears inebriated on walk home in early morning.

"Update. February 6, 2034. Subject One deceased. Cause of death: fall from highway overpass. Toxicology report showed blood alcohol level at .189. Ruled likely accident, possible self-harm."

She stared at the last sentence. Mike Coulson had been in his early twenties. Freya hadn't gotten to know all of the research participants, but she'd seen him in the waiting room at the clinic and had overheard him complaining to another patient about his job and how his dream was to be an actor. He didn't strike her as the suicidal type. His had been the first death.

She moved on to the next paragraph.

"Subject Two is a twelve-year-old male in good health. Attends middle school with higher-than-average grades. Not active in sports, but member of chess club, which meets each Thursday for an hour after school. Lives with father, a former car salesman, now disabled in late stages of colorectal cancer, his mother, a nurse who works the swing shift at a retirement home, and two siblings, both in elementary school. Residence is a hundred-year-old row house in Brooklyn, unsecured.

"Update. February 8, 2034. Subject Two deceased. Cause of death: House fire, smoke inhalation. Investigation reported no sign of arson, fire cause determined to be faulty wiring."

Freya's eyes teared up. The youngest person in the study had been Jase Prego. She'd spoken with him several times. He'd been an endearingly awkward pre-teen, and she suspected he'd had a crush on her. The memo didn't say as much, but she knew his entire family had died in that fire.

She didn't read the next several profiles; just scanned the words until she could note the age of the subject and moved on until she found her own age and gender.

"Subject Twelve is a seventeen-year-old female in good health. Attends public high school and maintains good grades. Active in school sports, but no extracurricular activities. No evidence of relationship. Lives with mother, a veterinarian who is also not currently in a relationship. Father deceased. No siblings. Residence is a rental unit in The Bronx. Building is secure. No vehicle registered to mother; subject and mother use public transportation."

Had they been planning to take out an entire city bus just to get to them? Deeply unsettled, Freya read on.

"Update. February 10, 2034. Surveillance unit report subjects exited residence at 4:22 pm yesterday with luggage and entered a black sedan with tinted windows, driver holo obtained, but FaceRecog negative. License plate [number redacted]. Unable to identify via DMV – possible law enforcement vehicle?"

February 10th had been the day they'd decided to leave the apartment they'd lived in for most of Freya's life and go on the run.

"Update. February 11, 2034. Subject and mother have not returned to residence. Workplace and school surveilled, but no sighting. Neighbors questioned; no knowledge of subject whereabouts. Bank account activity shows large cash withdrawal. Law enforcement sources have no information.

"Update. February 12, 2034. Friends/coworkers surveilled. No sighting of subject or mother. Moving company packed all furnishings and belongings into mobile storage units. Company was paid in advance for six months of storage.

"Update. February 13, 2034. Extended family surveilled. Two aunts, six uncles, twelve adult first and second cousins, all within New York State. Maternal grandfather in Maine. No sighting of subject or mother. Proceeding with FaceRecog, SpyWare, and SimClone."

Ryan had counseled them against showing their faces in public or contacting anyone via holophone, and he'd created a holomail account within the secure XIA network for them. At the time, Freya had been skeptical, thinking his measures were overkill, but now she realized he'd been right. How many times had she been tempted to break protocol and call her friends? Thankfully, she'd never done so.

"Update. February 14, 2034. Driver of vehicle noted in February 14th update identified: subject cousin, [name redacted], male, twenty-eight years-old, employment unknown. Brooklyn resident. Surveillance drone deployed.

"Update. February 15, 2034. Drone tracked subject cousin to suspected place of employment; cousin likely law enforcement, but access to records unavailable. All overt surveillance withdrawn.

"Update. February 16, 2034. No indication subject and mother scheduled to return. Bank account activity stagnant. FaceRecog produced multiple hits on both subject and mother in and around NYC, all "partials," indicating they are actively avoiding citywide cameras. SpyWare active on fourteen of twenty friend/family computers, and SimClone active on seventeen of twenty friend/family holophones. Intercepted messages and calls indicate most have no knowledge of subject or mother whereabouts, but a few do refer to them as being in hiding within the city.

"Update. February 17, 2034. SimClone hit. Call made to mother's friend from unregistered phone purchased at Brooklyn Fastmart. VoiceRecog identified caller as subject mother. Transcript of voice message: '[Redacted name], it's me. Meet me at the place and time we discussed. Be careful.' End transcript. Call origin triangulated within NYC. Surveillance unit one dispatched. Surveillance unit two dispatched to friend place of employment."

Freya's mother had risked discovery by making that one call to Mags – just so she could arrange for Freya to go back to school.

"Update. February 18, 2034. Surveillance unit one reports no sign of subject mother. Surveillance unit two reports no unusual activity, no additional contact between subject mother and friend.

"Update. February 21, 2034. Still no contact. Meeting 'place' may have been virtual. SpyWare active on subject mother's friend's home computer, but work computer inaccessible.

"Update. February 22, 2034. All efforts to locate subject and mother have failed. Team consensus is that subject and mother have been following avoidance protocol likely gotten from law enforcement relative, who has been positively identified as XIA agent. We must now exercise extreme caution. Evidence strongly suggests subject and mother are residing somewhere within NYC. Funds from cash withdrawal will not sustain them long. Mother will likely seek employment but will avoid veterinary field. Cannot discount possibility subject will reenter school system under an assumed name. Recommend proceed with Operation Predator."

Freya glanced up at Dan, shook her head, and muttered, "Operation Predator," before looking back down at the holo tablet.

"Update. April 11, 2034. Hit on Operation Predator questionnaire out of Manhattan. Surveillance unit dispatched to high school."

April 11th had been a week ago – the day before they'd run again. The behavior of that Trevor guy who'd stalked her suddenly made sense. He had to have been her last school's recipient of a Matrixeno graft.

"Update. April 12, 2034. Subject identified. Surveillance unit dispatched to home address, but no sighting. Neighbors questioned. Subject and mother 'on vacation,' – unlikely in middle of week. Were they tipped off, and if so, how?

"Update. April 19, 2034."

Yesterday, Freya thought.

"Another hit on Operation Predator questionnaire, this time out of Brooklyn. Surveillance unit dispatched to high school, but unit forced to retreat after confronted by police, who were called to investigate anonymous 911 call. 911 recording obtained. Transcript: 'Yeah, hello?' 'What's your emergency?' 'Um, yeah, there's these two guys in a silver car, parked down the street from [name of high school redacted]. Yeah, I just seen them try to get a girl into their car. She ran off, but the car's still there.' 'Did you get the license plate, sir?' 'Yeah, it's [number redacted]. Oh, man, there's another girl walking by. Yep, they're talking to her. She looks scared, too.' 'All right, sir, the police are on their way...sir? Are you there?' End transcript. VoiceRecog result indicates caller used voice altering software. Algorithm to unscramble running now. School is out, but surveillance drone scheduled to deploy tomorrow morning to perform FaceRecog on students."

Freya had reached the end of the document, but she continued to stare at the screen as she attempted to absorb everything.

Maddy had been watching over her shoulder. "What do you think?"

"I'm..." Freya had no words.

"Flabbergasted?" Maddy suggested.

"What'd it say?" Dan asked.

Freya looked at him in a daze. "That we were right to run. They *were* all murdered. And my mom and I were next."

Chapter Twenty

Dan's mind was still reeling from his inadvertent contribution to Freya's plight. He'd sensed something wasn't quite right with the questionnaire he'd been required to complete, but never would have guessed it had such a convoluted – and evil – purpose.

Freya handed the holo tablet back to Maddy, looking fragile as spun glass. She'd hardly touched her breakfast. He was on the verge of gently suggesting she finish eating when a woman's voice that seemed to come from within his skull blasted painfully, "Unidentified yacht. Prepare to be boarded."

Maddy winced and stuck a finger in her ear before turning to Freya. "That would be the cavalry." At Freya's blank look, she clarified, "Your cousin's here."

"How do you know?" Dan asked.

Maddy reached for a pair of dark sunglasses resting on a side table. "Let's just say I'm familiar with the XIA's methods." She gestured towards the door. "Shall we?"

Dan practically leapt out of his chair, but Freya got to her feet slowly, a cautious look on her face.

Maddy must have noticed, because as she settled the sunglasses on her face, she said, "I have no intention of getting into a pissing contest with them, so you can relax."

Freya didn't look convinced, but she followed Maddy out the door. Dan stayed close behind as they ascended the stairway to the top deck. The yacht was anchored just within a coastal inlet. The sea was calm, there wasn't a cloud in the sky, and the heat from the morning sun told him it would be a warm day. The land surrounding them on three sides appeared untouched by civilization. He saw no sign of the cavalry.

Maddy strolled across the deck and entered the bridge. An older man in a white suit – Dan assumed he was the captain – gestured to a console.

Maddy glanced at the holo displayed there and turned to look out the window towards the mouth of the inlet. She pasted a look of exaggerated resignation on her face and then marched out onto the deck with her hands held high like she was surrendering. Dan had no idea what was going on, but he was looking out at the horizon when an oddly shaped boat suddenly appeared out of nowhere.

Mouth open in surprise, he turned to Maddy, whose lips were pressed together in a poor attempt at hiding a smile.

"They call it a UAAV," she said, "which stands for Urban Something Something Vehicle."

"And it has, what? A cloaking device?" he asked.

"Essentially." Through the dark lenses of her sunglasses, he saw her eyes narrow in appreciation. "What I wouldn't give to get my hands on that tech."

"Wow," he said, genuinely impressed.

The UAAV slowly approached the yacht. It looked more like a large floating delivery van than a technologically advanced vehicle. When it was maybe thirty feet away, it turned parallel to the yacht. Through the open passenger side window, Dan saw a man looking through the sight of a rifle aimed at Maddy, but from this angle, he couldn't see the pilot. The sliding door on the side of the vehicle opened, revealing two more men, one dark-haired and one blonde. They were dressed in tactical gear, also holding rifles at the ready.

"Let her go, Maddy!" the dark-haired man shouted.

"You've got it all wrong, Dragila," Maddy shouted back. "I *rescued* her!"

"That's one way to put it," the man Maddy had called "Draheela" replied.

The blonde man called out, "You all right, Amanda?"

Freya responded, "I'm fine! Is Mom okay?"

He thrust a thumb up. "She's good!"

"Oh, come aboard already!" Maddy cried. "All this shouting is giving me a headache!"

"Not gonna happen," Dragila responded. "Just give us the girl and her friend."

"Okaaay!" Maddy drew the word out, like they were going to regret it. "But I've got a foolproof plan to catch daddy dearest in the act!"

Dan shot her a dubious look. If she was referring to her scheme to use Freya as bait, he wouldn't exactly call that foolproof. He didn't say anything, though. The Mad Eye queen had obviously been pouring on the charm this whole time, probably so Freya would trust her. If he publicly gainsaid her, he suspected she'd show her teeth.

She smiled at Freya and made a shooing motion with her hands. "To the outboard with you before they blast us to kingdom come!"

Maddy, Oscar, Freya, and Dan all piled into the outboard. Oscar started the motor and steered them towards the UAAV. Once they'd come alongside, the blonde man – Dan figured he must be Freya's cousin Ryan – held his hand out to Freya, but she didn't take it.

"Come on," Ryan said impatiently.

Freya bit her bottom lip and looked from Maddy to Ryan. "I think you should hear her out."

"What?" Ryan snapped. "Do you know who she *is*?"

"Yes, I do," Freya replied. "And I don't care. She *saved my life*. If she hadn't sent her people to find me, I'd be *dead* right now."

Dragila let out a short laugh. "Ahhh, this reeks of Maddy manipulation."

Maddy lifted her chin. "I'll have you know my father's the one doing the manipulating."

Dan thought he heard Dragila mutter, "Like father, like daughter," but Ryan's raised voice drowned him out.

"Amanda, get your ass in this vehicle *now*!"

"No!" Freya's face turned red in stubborn indignation. "The XIA left me and mom twisting in the wind. We've been living like scared little...*mole rats* this whole time."

"Yeah, well, things are gonna be different now. Your mother's at a safe house. You will be protected. Officially." Ryan's hand was still outstretched.

"In hiding?" Freya crossed her arms. "With another new name? I want my *life* back."

Ryan's arm dropped to his side. "And you think Maddy Singh's gonna get it for you?"

Freya looked at Maddy, who didn't miss a beat.

"We've worked well together in the past, haven't we?" she said to Dragila. "I can help the XIA catch my father, and Freya can stop running."

"What's in it for you?" The agent in the passenger seat asked.

"You were there, Cougar. You know what I want."

"We're not in the revenge game." Dragila's words were meant to discourage her, but Dan thought he saw a spark of interest in the man's eyes.

"Of course not," she replied flatly. "But you're under *siege* right now. By the time my father's lawyers are done with your organization...you won't have one."

Dragila turned to his companions to quietly confer. After a short conversation, he said, "I suppose you'll be asking for immunity?"

Maddy shrugged. "I wouldn't be averse to it."

"You tried to *kill* me."

"And Bryn," the young man behind the rifle in the passenger seat said.

Maddy shook her head. "No, I didn't. I knew the level of methane would never get high enough to give you so much as a headache. My engineers were brilliant, and they told me so. I also knew you'd break out. I didn't, however, realize that those plastic bullets Dillo was so enamored of would do so much damage. I *am* sorry about that."

Dragila's lips twisted like he wanted to refute her statement, but then he seemed to relent. "Fine. We'll talk."

Maddy inclined her head, all business now. "Please come aboard. As impressive as your UAAV is, it lacks certain amenities, like…space."

Ten minutes later, the heavily armed XIA agents, minus the UAAV pilot Dan still hadn't seen, stood in the sunshine on the top deck of the Phoenix. Maddy had dismissed the captain, but Oscar and Padme stayed close to their mistress. Oscar stood with his hands clasped in front of him in a deceptively relaxed stance, while Padme's expressive brown eyes seemed glued to the young man Maddy had referred to as Cougar. Dragila and Maddy sat at one end of the upholstered seating that curved around half of the deck, and Dan and Freya sank down onto the other end. Ryan hovered over Freya, silent and watchful. Cougar leaned against the railing near the stairs. His hands caught Dan's eye. The tips of the agent's fingers appeared to be covered in tan fur. It made sense that an XIA agent would have a xenograft, especially if he worked undercover. Dan remembered Wade telling him about an XBestia gang member – a grease fighter like Wade's dad Cerberus – who'd had cougar claws grafted onto his hands. Was this the same guy?

Freya nudged him, and he realized someone had asked him a question.

"I'm sorry, what?" he said.

"How did you get dragged into this?" Dragila asked.

"Oh, uh, I met Freya because my xenograft, apparently, makes me want to attack and—and eat her."

Dragila looked at him like he'd spoken Klingon. "What? Who's Freya?"

Dan glanced at Freya, who said, "I am. It's the name he knows me by."

Ryan stepped forward, scowling. "You attacked her?"

"No! I just—I wanted to. I mean…it's complicated. We figured out that my graft is from a snake that's *her* graft's natural predator."

"Huh," Dragila said, nodding thoughtfully. "Some grafts do influence the host in unusual ways. But what I was asking for was a blow by blow of the events that led you here."

"Ah," Dan said with an embarrassed little laugh. "Sorry. Sleep deprived."

After that, he and Freya filled the agents in on what had happened. Dragila, who listened intently but seemed unimpressed by their adventure, became keenly interested when Dan told them about the questionnaire. When Maddy mentioned Matrixeno, Dragila fired questions at her, and as she answered them, Dan got the distinct impression she was gratified by his intensity.

Once the agents had been apprised of the situation, Dragila lifted his eyebrows at Maddy. "So what's this ingenious plan of yours?"

Chapter Twenty-one

"I asked myself what was the most important thing to my father," Maddy replied.

"Money," Cougar said.

"Yes, but his funds are untouchable, believe me I've tried."

"What then?" Dragila asked. Freya could tell he was getting exasperated.

"Image," Maddy said. "Reputation. He's put tremendous effort into creating a public persona that makes him seem like the Dalai Lama. At the same time, his private persona, the one he unleashes around his business associates – as well as certain family members who don't fall within the narrow confines of what he considers acceptable sexual orientation – is that of a ruthless, cold-blooded, corrupt, wretched little man."

"Tell us how you *really* feel," Dragila said.

Maddy rebuked him with a sour look before continuing. "As you know, my father relies heavily on his soldiers to do his dirty work."

"Obviously," Dragila said.

"We'll need an extraordinary incentive to coax him into getting personally involved, especially since the last time he took a hands-on approach, it didn't go so well for him. And it's imperative he doesn't suspect the XIA is involved."

"Again, stating the obvious. What. Is. Your. Plan?"

Freya saw Maddy's mouth tighten in anger, but she just shrugged. "We get him to commit a crime in front of witnesses who can't be coerced or paid to stay silent."

Ryan let out a short, derisive laugh. "That's entrapment. That's the actual *definition* of entrapment."

"No," Maddy retorted. "It isn't. It's only entrapment if it's a crime he wouldn't normally commit. You see? I know the difference. And don't try to tell me the XIA has never resorted to such methods." Dragila was the recipient of another of her withering looks.

"We don't have as much latitude these days, thanks in great part to your father's lawsuit," he said. "Even a whiff of impropriety and his lawyers will sense chum in the water. Besides, that public persona you mentioned works against us. No one would believe he's capable of a fraction of the things he's done."

"That's why we have to go all 'Mission Impossible' on him," Maddy said.

Dragila chuckled, and despite his earlier exasperation, Freya suspected he was actually fond of the Mad Eye queen.

"I appreciate your enthusiasm and willingness to help," he said, "but your plan's extremely thin."

"Well, as soon as you showed up, I had to bin my original plan and come up with a new one on the fly. I admit it needs some fleshing out."

Freya expected someone to ask about Maddy's original plan – the one where Freya was supposed to have been dangled as bait – but no one did. It seemed as if Dragila was about to flush Maddy's half-baked scheme down the toilet, but then he said, "We *might* be able to help you, or more accurately, help you help us."

Maddy smiled. "Now that's what I'm talking about."

Dragila's brown eyes rolled briefly upward. "What can you tell us about your father that we don't already know?"

Maddy gestured with a flourish. "Meet Oscar DeSantia, formerly a member of my father's inner circle."

Oscar tilted his head slightly to one side, but otherwise remained still.

"You look familiar." It was Cougar.

"He should," Maddy said. "You saved his life."

Oscar stepped over to Cougar, hand extended. "I was on Singh's yacht."

Cougar shook his hand but looked confused.

"I jumped overboard after you all blew up the helicopter," Oscar said.

Cougar grimaced. "Cold, wasn't it?"

"Like a witch's tit," Oscar replied.

"So how did I save your life?"

"Singh and his men made it to the dock, but I don't swim so well. I got close, but my muscles cramped up something fierce. I called out for help, and you tossed me a life vest. Woulda gone under for sure if wasn't for that."

Maddy picked up the thread of the story. "You may recall that after you took my father away, you left his men, including Oscar, on the dock, unsecured. In the chaos following that disastrous attempt to break through the army barrier, they captured me. When the first of the civilian rescuers showed up, they forced me to go with them. In exchange for my life, I had only one bargaining chip: the printer."

Freya noticed that every one of the XIA agents perked up considerably. She knew from Ryan that the printer had been a small, state-of-the-art portable 3D version capable of producing nanoscale electronics. Its hard drive was purported to contain Nicolas Fournier, The Bestia Butcher's nanoneuron program, as well as information that would implicate Singh in a multitude of crimes. It had last been in the custody of the director of the XIA, who was transporting it to the District Attorney. His vehicle had been attacked en route, he'd been critically injured, and the printer along with a prisoner named Savvy, had disappeared.

"So you're responsible for the assault on Deputy Director Unger." Dragila's voice was dangerously low. "He barely survived."

"I wasn't *there*; I didn't participate other than to tell them about it. I had no choice. They were going to kill me unless I proved useful."

"I can vouch for that," Oscar said.

"How did you know where the printer was?" Dragila asked, before making a face and saying, "Oh, right. The tracking device installed on your phone. Damn it. I don't suppose you still have that phone?"

"If I did, we wouldn't be here. As it was, the only reason Savvy and I escaped is because I convinced Oscar to defect."

"She can be persuasive," Oscar said.

"That she can," Dragila replied.

"Did he destroy it? The printer?" Ryan asked.

"I was assigned to guard her while the others took care of that." Oscar glanced at Maddy with something akin to hero worship in his eyes. "I doubt Singh destroyed it, though. He woulda wanted to find out what Fournier had on him, plus everyone knew he wanted to git his mitts on that nanoneuron tech."

Freya looked at Cougar. His claws were more than just a graft; he was able to open and close them because he'd had nanoneurons implanted in his brain that controlled the claws' motor functions.

"As did we all," Maddy said. "Especially after that insane demonstration at Fournier's farm."

Freya didn't know what Maddy was referring to, but Ryan *had* mentioned that the nanoneurons could essentially be used as mind control, a frightening concept.

"So you have no idea where it might be now?" Dragila asked.

Both Maddy and Oscar shook their heads, but Maddy said, "We looked. My father is skittish. Prefers to live on his yacht – the new one now, obviously – but it won't be there. Keeps his legitimate business strictly separate from his criminal dealings. Oscar knew about an abandoned building in the city, a Hyena den where his soldiers and cyberexploiters were squatting, but as soon as we got close, they vacated and literally burned the entire building to the ground to destroy any evidence."

"It's protocol if security's breached," Oscar said. "Singh don't take no chances."

"What about the pier?" Dragila asked. "Can you corroborate that it was blown up on his orders?"

Oscar let out a small laugh. "I'll tell ya what I can right here, right now, but just so ya know, there's no way I'm testifying. That would be plain stupid."

Dragila hesitated, but then nodded.

"Heard him make the call myself," Oscar said.

"Who'd he call?" Ryan asked.

"Dunno."

"That wasn't the original plan anyway," Maddy said. "Poppy's Pier belonged to the city. Remember, Dragila, that you told me he was influencing politicians? I think that was the reason the pier was never repaired. As long as it was an eyesore it kept neighboring property prices down. That way, he and his cronies could snap them up for a bargain as soon as they came on the market. It's not like my father to sacrifice a lucrative scam unless he's cornered, or the payoff is too big to resist. That night, however, things did not go as expected."

"Congressman Abbott," Dragila said.

"Yes." Maddy looked at Oscar, who said, "The hit was supposed to happen at the airport, but Abbott changed plans at the last minute."

"Why bring him to the pier?"

"Riots messed everything up," Oscar replied, "The army was thick on the ground and the hitmen had to wing it. Lucky for Singh, he had a high-ranking officer in his pocket."

"Who?"

"Dunno," Oscar said again with a headshake. "He didn't exactly confide in his employees."

Freya, like everyone else, had seen the holocast Bryn Vega made on the pier. Bryn's warning that it was wired to blow had saved countless lives. Part of the holocast included a statement by Philip Singh – one he'd made clear was coerced out of him. Singh denied having anything to do with the plot, and once he and the rest of the people who'd ended up on Poppy's Pier were safe, used the holocast against the XIA in his lawsuit.

"Anything else? Maybe some actionable intel?" Dragila opened his mouth to say something else, but then he frowned suddenly, head turning in such a way that Freya knew he was listening to something through his earbug.

"ETA?" he asked, as the body language of the other agents abruptly changed from relaxed to alert.

"What is it?" Maddy asked.

"We got incoming, approaching rapidly," Cougar replied, "UAAV's got two boats on radar, and our drone picked up four vehicles on land."

Dragila turned to Maddy, upper lip lifted in a snarl. "Anything you want to tell us?"

Her face revealed a tinge of regret. "I admit, I was hoping to get his attention by bringing Freya aboard. Obviously, I didn't know you were going to be here."

Dragila let out a snort of derision but didn't waste any more time with recrimination. "What are your defense capabilities?"

"Formidable," Maddy said sternly. She glanced at Freya and Dan. "But *they're* safer elsewhere."

"Now it occurs to you?" Ryan snapped.

Dragila lifted his chin at him, and Ryan grabbed Freya's upper arm and urged her to her feet. "Let's move!"

On the way down the narrow stairwell, they had to squeeze to one side to allow three armed crewmembers to rush past on their way up. Judging by their appearance, the crew were xenos, and to Freya, looked like nothing less than modern-day pirates.

Once she reached the bathing platform, she and Dan jumped into the outboard while Ryan untied it. Then he leaped aboard, started the boat, and shifted into gear so rapidly the nose of the small craft lifted as it surged forward.

Freya gripped the edges of the hard-plastic seat and looked around for the UAAV, but it had gone invisible again. The ocean horizon beyond the mouth of the inlet was devoid of watercraft, and she couldn't discern whether there were any roads or paths on the rocky coastline. She knew Singh's soldiers were coming, but so far there was no sign of them. Other than the steady rumble of the outboard's motor, the peaceful vista seemed ominously quiet.

Ryan beached them on a narrow stretch of sand and hustled Freya and Dan out. He pointed to a craggy bluff protruding from a sandbank. "There. Hide!"

"What are you–?" Freya started to ask.

"Right behind you," he interrupted. "Go!"

Freya and Dan sprinted for the bluff. When they reached it, they dropped to their hands and knees and crawled under a crumbling outcrop. From that dark space, she saw the outboard speeding back towards the yacht. She started to crawl back out, but Dan grabbed her wrist to stop her. A man had come into view, walking towards the water. He was dressed in military fatigues and held what she instantly recognized as a rocket launcher balanced on one shoulder. She looked back at the outboard, but if Ryan was aboard, he was ducking down to make himself a smaller target.

With a loud *bang*, the little rocket shot out across the water so stunningly fast she barely had time to gasp before it hit its target. A plume of water obscured the outboard before raining down on the destruction.

Dan wrapped his arms around her from behind, one hand clamping down over her mouth. Her instinct was to struggle, but then another man joined the first on the beach. He looked down and pointed at the sand. With a thrill of terror, she realized she and Dan had left a trail of footprints on the pristine beach leading directly to their hiding place. The first man set the rocket launcher on the sand and pulled a handgun from his shoulder holster. Freya and Dan shrank back into the shadows as the men started towards them, but then a rapid series of pops sounded. Both men jerked and fell, and she saw Ryan behind them running through the light surf, soaking wet, gun in hand. He'd cleverly sent the outboard off unmanned while he lay in wait submersed in the ocean.

Freya let out a cry of relief, but their deliverance was short-lived. Ryan had reached the two downed men and she expected him to run past them, but instead, he stopped short and lifted his arms above his head. He was maybe fifty yards away, and it was hard to tell, but she was pretty sure the men he'd shot were down for the count. Which meant he was surrendering to someone else – someone she couldn't see from her vantage point.

"Hey," Dan whispered, tugging on her sleeve. "Look."

She tore her gaze away from Ryan, wanting and not wanting to watch whatever was going to happen next. Dan tilted his head towards the back of their hidey hole. Her eyes had adjusted to the darkness enough to see that they were hunkering in the entrance to a low, deep cavern that had been carved from under the rock by the sea. A pinprick light source far back into the recesses indicated a potential alternate exit route.

She looked back at Ryan, who had turned away from them as if he didn't want to give their location away. His captives had come into view. The taller of the two was a woman with short brown hair. Her male

95

companion held a black rifle with a long, curved clip protruding from the bottom. Freya didn't know much about guns, but anyone who watched holovision knew a semiautomatic weapon when they saw one.

"We can't help him," Dan said quietly. "And if we stay here, they'll find us."

She knew it was true, and also knew Ryan would want her to keep running. She clenched her jaw to keep the tears in her eyes from falling and began crawling deeper into the cavern. The sandy rock beneath her hands and knees was cold, the moist air redolent with the odor of fish and rotting sea vegetation. The massive bluff above her should have produced a claustrophobic sense of impending doom, but she found its presence almost comforting. As she scrambled along, she wondered if that was more evidence that her graft was influencing her. A naked mole rat would certainly be at home in this environment.

Sounds from outside reached them; rapid pops and deep booms that shook the sand loose from the slab above them. Even dulled by the insulating properties of rock and earth, the noises were terrifying.

She and Dan crawled for maybe twenty yards. The ground sloped gently downward to the far end of the cavern. There, the cavern opened up, the ceiling slanting sharply upward into a narrow space where they could stand upright with plenty of room to spare. The lower half of this section was solid stone, eroded by the sea like the rest of the cavern, but the top portion of the back wall consisted of packed dirt and rocks. A thin shaft of sunlight shone through a crumbling, vertical fissure about four inches wide that started several feet off the ground and extended to the top of the cavern – an opening much too small for them to escape through.

"Hey!" someone shouted.

Freya ducked down to look back the way they'd come. The man who'd captured Ryan was squatting at the opening of the cavern, weapon resting on his knees. Next to him, she saw the bottom half of the woman's khakis. Ryan was nowhere in sight.

"Come out of there!" the woman called.

"Yeah, right," Dan muttered. He nudged Freya. "Get out of the light. You're an easy target."

She moved to stand as far back as possible, pressing her back against the cavern wall. When she and Dan didn't respond, the man must have decided there'd been enough discussion. He fired a short burst of gunfire, and instantly the rock near her knee shattered as the whine of a ricochet echoed through the cavern.

"Watch it!" the woman snapped. "That almost hit me!"

"Yes, Matron. Sorry, Matron!" the man replied.

96

Freya couldn't hear most of the woman's response, but then she caught the word, "grenade."

She stared at Dan, whose face mirrored her shock and dismay.

Chapter Twenty-two

Dan's first thought was to escape. He turned to the back wall of the cave and pressed his face to the fissure, squinting into the light to see how deep it was. Curling his fingers around the edge, he easily dislodged a sandy chunk of sod. Just as it occurred to him that it wouldn't take long for them to dig their way out, the distinct clink of metal on rock sent a surge of adrenaline coursing through his system. Hologames had taught him there were several kinds of grenades, some designed to kill, others to disable or flush out quarry. He wasn't going to passively wait to find out which version was on its way. He spun around and dropped into a crouch, hoping the grenade would hit one of the many rocky obstacles in the cavern and stop well short of their position.

It didn't.

The next few seconds were a blur. "Take cover!" he yelled as the olive-green orb bounced right into his waiting hands. He made a split-second decision and lunged for the back wall, shoving his hand elbow-deep into the fissure and wedging the grenade into it. He barely had time to hurl himself to the ground before it blew.

The explosion was a deafening, concussive shock that pelted his back with projectiles.

Definitely the deadly kind, he thought.

The cavern filled with dust and smoke, and he choked on it until it occurred to him to pull his shirt up over his nose. After he caught his breath, he got up onto his hands and knees and looked around dazedly. Freya was curled into a ball in the corner, hands folded protectively over her neck.

"You okay?" He barely heard his own voice over the ringing in his ears.

She lifted her head, hair saturated with dirt. "I think so."

The fissure was now a chest-high gaping hole about four feet deep. He stood, legs shaking. "Let's get out of here."

She staggered to the hole, and he laced his fingers together and bent over so she could place her foot into the cradle. After he hoisted her up, she crawled through to the other side.

"See anything?" he asked.

"All clear," she replied. "But it's a bit of a drop."

She maneuvered herself into a sitting position with her legs hanging out, and then rolled over facing him. He levered himself up into the hole and offered her his hands. She took them, gave him a look of worried determination, and slid backwards. He stretched out onto his stomach as far as he could, his upper body hanging partially out over a ravine. As soon as he saw the "bit of a drop" he knew it was too far, but when he tried to pull her back, she said, "Let go! It'll be fine."

He took a second look, noting that the sand dune making up the side of the ravine was slanted. She would hit the incline after a short drop, and then would be able to slide the rest of the way. Not without trepidation, he released her. As he'd hoped, she slid rapidly down. He quickly followed, descending feet first.

Freya was sitting at the bottom of the ravine, examining her hand.

"Are you hurt?" he asked.

"I'm fine."

He could see she was bleeding, but they didn't have time to nurse their wounds. Assuming the bad guys sent someone into the cavern to verify their demise, it would soon be obvious they'd escaped.

According to the sounds coming from beyond the dunes, the dynamic of the conflict had changed. No longer a furious exchange of gunfire and heavy weaponry, now they heard shouting punctuated by the occasional gunshot.

He gestured to the far side of the ravine and she nodded. They beat their way through the thick seagrass at the very bottom, and then climbed the far side, which wasn't nearly as steep as the drop they'd made. When they reached the top, they lay flat and cautiously peered over. There were four identical black SUVs parked haphazardly along the side of a roughly graded gravel road. A heavyset older man stood guard about twenty yards away, luckily not facing in their direction.

They ducked out of sight and Dan rested his forehead on folded arms. "What do we–?" he started to say.

"There they are!" someone yelled. He twisted around and saw the man who'd captured Ryan leaning out of the grenade hole. Dan expected him to start shooting, but instead he pulled back into the cavern, and when Dan heard the crunch of boots on gravel, he realized it was because the guard was heading their way and the man didn't want to risk hitting his comrade.

"Oh, *crap!*" Freya whispered.

"You go right, I go left – on three," he said. She grimaced, eyes eloquently terrified, but dipped her head in acknowledgement.

Quietly, he counted, listening as the guard got closer. He curled his fingers into the sand, grabbing a handful. As he uttered the word "Three!" he made a break for it, barreling up and over the lip of the ravine ahead of Freya. The guard was right there, less than ten feet away. He reached for his shoulder holster, but Dan rushed him, hurling the sand into his startled face. Before the guard could do more than raise a hand to his eyes, Dan slammed a shoulder into his soft gut. The guard merely grunted, wrapping his arms around Dan and pulling him backwards into a crushing hug. Dan tried to break loose, but under all that fat, the guard was strong.

Dan knew nothing about wrestling and struggling wasn't working. His arms were pinned to his sides, and the guard's punishing grip was making it hard to breathe. He threw his head back in an attempted head-butt, but only managed a glancing blow to the guard's chin.

"Ya little shit," the guard growled, breath reeking of garlic. "Ima squish ya like a bug."

Dan's vision was beginning to black out around the edges when the guard suddenly sagged – out of the corner of his eye Dan could see Freya's hand and surmised correctly that she'd leapt upon the guard's back. Dan took advantage of the momentary distraction to twist his torso violently, managing to get his right arm free. He had just wrapped his hand around the hilt of the guard's gun when he heard a thud and the man dropped like a stone, taking Freya with him.

Behind them stood Ryan holding a rock in his fist. The agent bent and began patting the guard down. He shoved his hand into the man's pants pocket, withdrawing an electronic key. Then he grabbed the man's hand and pressed his thumb onto the keypad. One of the SUVs roared to life.

Ryan dropped the guard's hand, but then his eyes narrowed, and he picked it back up again. He grasped the man's wrist and shoved his shirtsleeve up to reveal a xenograft – a patch of tan fur with two dark spots.

"Clan submissive," he said, and made a disgusted face. He dropped the man's arm and stood.

Dan was busy filling his lungs with oxygen, so he didn't react when Ryan took the gun out of his slack hand.

Ryan tossed the key to Freya. "Take it. I'll disable the other vehicles."

"We're not going to *leave* you here," Freya said.

"Yeah," Ryan growled. "You are. As soon as you get somewhere safe, dump the SUV and get as far away as possible. Go!"

Freya's jaw was set stubbornly, so Dan grabbed her wrist and pulled her away. She tossed one last anguished look over her shoulder at Ryan, and then she and Dan sprinted to the SUV. They both reached for the passenger door handle.

"I don't know how to drive," she said.

Dan hadn't driven a car since last year's Driver's Ed course. The riots had interrupted his plans for taking ownership his dad's old work truck. They'd had to sell it along with the house in order to pay the medical bills.

He ran around the SUV and climbed into the driver's seat. As soon as he shut the door, the Navoice reminded him to put his seatbelt on. He did so, and then stared at the controls, which looked nothing like his dad's older model truck.

"What's wrong?" Freya asked.

"Nothing," he muttered.

"Let's go."

"Alright." He pressed his foot to the brake and looked for the gear shift. "I just...how do I put it in drive?"

The Navoice asked, "Would you like to put the vehicle in drive?"

"Yes," he responded.

There was an almost indistinguishable change to the sound of the motor. Dan took his foot off the brake and the SUV slowly moved forward. He shifted his foot to the electrigas pedal and pressed down gently as he turned the wheel.

"You drive like a granny," Freya said.

He responded by putting more pressure on the pedal, and the SUV surged up the hill, tires briefly losing traction in the gravel. He glanced in the rearview mirror and saw Ryan squatting next to the back wheel of one of the other vehicles as he punctured a tire. The SUV crested the rise and he caught a glimpse of Maddy's yacht and two other boats, all spewing black plumes of smoke into the air. A jet of water arced across the blue sky out of nowhere – the pilot of the UAAV must be attempting to put out the fire on Maddy's yacht.

As Dan turned onto a deserted two-lane road, he fought a sense of panic brought on by the horrific realization that he'd just narrowly escaped death.

Chapter Twenty-three

Freya sat twisted in her seat, watching out the back window in case someone followed them. Ryan had told them to get somewhere safe and dump the SUV, but she had no idea where "safe" might be. In fact, she had no idea where they even were. All Maddy had said was that she'd taken the yacht further up the coast.

As if he'd read her thoughts, Dan said, "Where we are?"

Freya opened her mouth to respond, but the Navoice beat her to it. "Would you like to view Holomaps?"

"Yes," Dan replied.

A holo of the coast of Connecticut appeared above the center console, with a little red pin marking their location.

"Would you like to input your destination?" Navoice asked.

"No!" Freya said. Then to clarify her outburst, "They might be able to use that to track us."

"This car's got all the bells and whistles," he said. "As soon as they figure out we took it, they'll be able to track us regardless."

"So when we dump it, we need to get as far away from it as quickly as possible."

"Which means we either take a bus or hitchhike."

She sighed. "We'd be sitting ducks on a bus."

"I don't have any money for a ticket anyway. You?"

She shook her head.

"Hitchhiking it is," he said.

"But what if no one picks us up? We could totally be standing on the side of the road with our thumbs out when Singh's soldiers show up."

He turned right onto another road. The terrain out the window quickly changed from wild and empty to a neighborhood populated with mansions overlooking huge tracts of pristinely groomed land.

"Maybe if we destroy it? Like burn it or drive it into a lake?"

She looked down at the gash on her hand and mumbled, "Probably get caught in the act by the local cops."

"You gonna shoot down all my suggestions?"

"Come up with one that'll work."

His only response was a short exhale out his nose.

He turned onto a main road and they drove for some time in uneasy silence. They passed a speed limit sign and she noticed he was going about ten miles per hour too fast but didn't comment. Getting pulled over for speeding would be bad but getting caught for not running fast enough would be much worse.

"We'll head for home," he said. "It'll be easier to hide in the city."

She studied the Holomap. "Problem is finding a route without a toll."

"Check the glove compartment. Maybe there's some cash."

Freya pressed the latch and the glovebox popped open. "Well," she said, "there's a vehicle user's manual and a gun."

Dan glanced away from the road long enough to get a quick look at the gun. "Cool. Ever use one?"

"Ryan taught me. You?"

He shook his head. "Never had the occasion."

She took the gun out and examined it. Technically, Ryan had *showed* her how to use a gun, but she'd never fired one. This one was loaded, and the safety was off. She flipped it to "on" and tucked the gun into the pocket of her coat.

The further they got from the ocean, the less affluent the neighborhood. They followed the Holomap to a main highway but hadn't been on it very long when the Navoice informed them that they were low on electrigas. Dan swore under his breath and swerved towards an off ramp.

"We have to dump it here," he said.

Once he'd exited, he adjusted his speed on the main road through what appeared to be a small rural town, stopping at a flashing yellow sign to let a rowdy group of high schoolers cross the street.

"Is it lunchtime?" she asked.

The Navoice answered, "The time is eleven thirty-eight."

The last two students in the group were holding hands as they sauntered across the tarmac, enjoying the sunshine and each other's company. Freya envied them the normalcy. She looked at Dan, whose lips were thin as he impatiently waited for the couple to cross.

"You okay?" she asked.

"Hungry," he said, giving her a meaningful glance.

The high school kids were congregating around the outdoor tables at a local café, and the scent of grilled meat coming through the cracked SUVs windows was mouth-watering. The next block up, they drove past the local fire station.

"Wait!" Freya exclaimed. "This is perfect."

"What do you mean?"

"Right here. In front of the fire station. Park in the driveway and ditch. They'll have to have it towed."

"Which means we won't be anywhere near it when the soldiers come for it."

"Exactly," she said. "Eventually they'll pinpoint where we dumped it, but we'll gain ourselves some time."

He smiled at her. "Good idea."

"Thanks."

Dan circled the block, and then pulled into the wide driveway in front of the station. All seemed quiet.

"I'm gonna leave the keys in it," he said. "They can't start it without an authorized thumbprint."

She nodded and jumped out, gun heavy in her pocket. He came around and they walked swiftly away. At the end of the block, she began to relax as no one chased them down.

"Now what?" she asked.

"I gotta eat."

"With what money?"

He nodded in the direction of the café. "Dine and dash?"

"Too risky," she said. "And seriously not my style."

"Then what?"

"Just blend in. We'll think of something."

"Hold on." He waved a hand in her general direction. "You're...filthy."

She suffered a brief flashback to the explosion in the cave, and for a moment couldn't seem to breathe. The thick dust and dirt that had filled the cavern had been suffocating.

She swallowed, mouth suddenly dry as a desert, but said with effort, "You're not exactly spotless yourself."

"Didn't say I was." His response sounded more defensive than she thought was warranted, but then again, his hunger was probably nagging at him.

She bent at the waist and ran her fingers through her hair while Dan shook his head like a dog. Then they brushed their hands across the worst of the dirt on their clothing. She directed him to turn around so she could get his back, but when it came time to return the favor, he balked.

"I can't," he said, taking a step backward.

"Fine. It's fine." She removed her coat and brushed at it herself. Once it looked presentable, she put it back on and said, "Let's go."

When they reached the café, they stopped at the corner of the building and leaned against the wall near the garbage can. They pretended to talk while surreptitiously eyeing the occupied tables. Out of habit, Freya kept her head down to avoid any possible street cameras. After a while, the kids began to leave. Lunch hour was over. Most of them left their trays on the tables, but then a group of three girls pushed back their chairs and walked towards the garbage can. None of the girls had finished their food and were about to dump it all when Dan moved to intercept them.

"Hi," he said with a slow grin.

The girls gaped at the handsome stranger. He held out a hand. "I'll take those for you."

As if he'd flipped a switch, the girls blushed and giggled and handed over their trays like simpering fools. Freya rolled her eyes. With an apologetic smile, Dan turned his back on them, ostensibly to empty the trays into the garbage, but the girls seemed loath to leave the vicinity. Freya figured his plan was to keep some of the food, but with the girls watching his every move, he'd be too proud. She sauntered over and one by one, gave each girl the stink eye. Then she slid her hand around Dan's waist.

"You're such a gentleman, sweetheart," she said. She sensed rather than felt him subtly stiffen, and she backed off a bit. As expected, the girls suddenly remembered they had to get back to class. Freya helped Dan consolidate the leftover French fries into one container and wrap up two half-eaten hamburgers.

"Sweetheart?" he said, giving her a sidelong look.

"They needed motivation to leave."

"Oh, okay, you weren't jealous or anything."

"Not at all."

With their dubious lunch in hand, they continued walking. She delicately nibbled on her burger, careful to avoid the bitten spots, while he shoved burger and fries into his mouth indiscriminately. He caught her watching his progress out of the corner of her eyes and laughed at himself.

"Not pretty, huh?"

"You certainly eat with…gusto."

He shrugged. "Better than chowing down on you."

Before she could respond, he said, "That didn't come out right."

"No." She made a sardonic face at him. "It didn't." Then after a moment, "You don't really want to actually *bite* me, do you?"

He stopped. "The truth? Feels like I want to…own you, body and soul."

It was a dramatic, overly poetic thing for a guy to say, which was why Freya didn't doubt for a second that he meant every word. She tried to take it at face value: he wasn't telling her that he cared for her, he was saying he wanted to possess her. Like a thing – or in this case, like a favorite snack he didn't want to share.

There was a city park up ahead, a green swath of grass with huge old maple trees surrounding a derelict-looking play structure. Although it was a little chilly out, it was a beautiful day, but there was no one in the park enjoying it. Dan seemed intent on passing it by, but Freya veered onto the grass and headed for a garbage can. She wadded up the burger wrappers and tossed them in. Dan spotted a water faucet and bent to get a drink.

There was an odd sound when the stream of water began trickling down the drain, like a faint whirring. When Dan lifted his head and let go of the button, the sound didn't go away.

"You hear that?" she asked.

"Yeah, sounds like a…" he squinted up at the sky.

She followed his gaze but saw nothing. "A what?"

Just as he uttered the word, "Drone," the air about ten feet above them shimmered, and it appeared.

Chapter Twenty-four

Dan thought Singh's soldiers had found them, but then a voice came from the hovering drone. "Mandy."

"Ryan!" Freya exclaimed. "Thank goodness you're okay! How'd you find us?"

"We captured one of Singh's men and persuaded him to talk. The grenade they hit you with was filled with nanotech – micro transmitters that stick to your clothes like a burr – so if the blast doesn't kill you, they can still track you. They had a drone following you, but we took it out. *Our* drone picked up a convoy headed this way, about fifteen minutes out. The nanotech is solar powered, so you need to get out of the sun and dump your clothes...fast."

"Are you coming to get us?"

"Can't. The UAAV took heavy damage. I'm still in the thick of the aftermath. I don't know when I'll be able to get away. Find somewhere safe and wait."

"Okay, but...where is safe? And how long should we wait?"

"Try to make it back to the city, but don't go home – neither of you. Don't contact the police and stay away from XIA headquarters. We're trying to get control of the agency back, but our countermeasures have been hamstrung by someone on the inside. Be careful. Now go!" The drone disappeared.

Freya looked at Dan, eyes wide, and he briefly scanned the area.

"That way!" He pointed past the play structure, where a decorative wooden bridge spanned a creek.

They sprinted across the grass. At the bank of the creek, he stripped off his hoodie and shirt and dropped them into the brackish water. Freya took the gun out of her pocket, set it on a rock, and removed her coat. She hesitated, so he took the coat out of her hands and tossed it in. The current took it slowly downstream.

As he was unbuttoning his jeans, she asked, "What about our hair?" and he realized she was right. Stripping down wouldn't matter if the nanotech was in their hair and maybe even on their skin. Ryan had advised them to get out of the sun, but that didn't mean the micro transmitters would instantly stop working. More likely, the sun's charge would last even in the shade – for how long, he had no way of knowing.

"We wash it off." He stepped onto rocks slippery with green algae and waded into the center of the creek. The water was cold, but not deep; it only came to a few inches above his knees. He sat abruptly, submerging himself up to his chest, and as he pulled his shoes and socks off, tossed over his shoulder, "Come on!"

He heard splashing, but concentrated on yanking his sodden jeans off, thinking he should have done it before he'd taken the plunge. He removed everything but his jockey shorts, and then ducked his head under and rubbed his hair vigorously. When his scalp began to hurt from the rough treatment, he stopped and rolled over in the water. Freya, soaking wet and dressed only in a black sports bra and matching boy cut briefs, had finished before him and was standing on the shore by the gun, arms folded self-consciously across her abdomen. The sunlight slanting down on her skin highlighted a multitude of fine body hairs lifted by chill bumps.

She said something, but the words got lost in the turmoil somewhere between his ears and his brain. He'd seen plenty of girls wearing bikinis more revealing than her undergarments, and yet something about the vulnerable way she was looking at him set fire to his hunger. He was glad he hadn't risen from the water, because there was no way his jockey shorts could conceal his reaction from her. He silently cursed himself as he twisted around to face the opposite direction.

Assuming she'd said something along the lines of, "What now?" he responded, "We find shelter."

"Right," her tone indicated he'd gotten it wrong. "Did you even hear me?"

"I got water in my ears," he muttered.

"I said we should head for the fence."

He stood, keeping his back to her as he checked out the long line of fencing parallel to the creek. From his vantage point, he couldn't see into any of the yards, but unlike newer neighborhoods where the fencing was all one construction, these were built individually, so it was easy to distinguish one yard from another. Older houses meant less security. About four yards up, a sign posted on a wooden gate read, "For Rent."

"That one." He pointed. "Might be empty."

She picked up the gun and held it like she was attempting to conceal it in her hands, for lack of anywhere else to hide it.

They crossed the bridge and took a thin dirt path along the fence line. Dan's feet were unprotected by callouses after a summer spent wearing sneakers in the city, and he flinched every time he stepped on a rock. The gate wasn't closed; it had been deliberately propped open with a cinder block. He looked around the park to make sure no one was watching, and then they slipped into the yard. As they cautiously approached the house, he paid little attention to the backyard with its patchy grass and scruffy bushes, instead focusing on the sliding glass door. Through the window, past blinds that had been opened to let in the light, he peered inside at what looked to be the living room.

"No furniture." He pushed against the handle, surprised when the door slid open.

They went inside, and he closed the door and rotated the blinds closed.

Freya released a heavy, relieved sigh. "I guess we hunker down again."

Dan thought he heard something, so he raised a hand. Faint, repetitive, high-pitched noises were coming from upstairs.

"Is that a cat?" she whispered with a concerned frown between her brows.

He padded across the carpet towards the staircase, wincing at every creak of the floorboards. As soon as he caught sight of the clothes and shoes strewn haphazardly on the steps, he realized what the sounds were. Earlier, he'd noticed Freya watching that couple holding hands as they crossed the street. He recognized the jacket on the stairs as belonging to the male half of the couple, who, it appeared, was right now upstairs coaxing some intense sounds out of his girlfriend.

Freya came up next to him and when she saw the clothes, clapped her hands over her mouth to muffle her laughter.

He started to back away, but she nudged him and gestured to the clothes. His head went back in understanding. They quickly gathered everything but the underwear and took the bundles into the kitchen. Freya dressed in a light sweater, jeans, and flat shoes, all of which looked slightly too big for her. Luckily for Dan, the guy wore the same size tennis shoes and his shorts had an elastic waist, so fit wasn't an issue. When he put the jacket on, he found a holophone in the pocket. He held it up to show her, and she whispered, "Leave it. I'm sure it's password protected. Besides, they'll need it to call someone for new clothes."

She handed him the gun and he tucked it in the pocket, which wasn't quite roomy enough to completely hide it.

They exited through the front door and walked away at a fast pace, but not fast enough to attract attention.

As they walked, Freya let out the occasional snigger.

"Found that pretty amusing, huh?" he asked.

"I honestly thought a cat had gotten trapped in one of the rooms."

He laughed. "Imagine if you'd gone up there to rescue it."

Her cheeks turned pink and she shook her head. After a moment, she said, "I hope we didn't just ruin their lives."

"They'll get over it. A little embarrassment for them, life and death for us. No comparison."

The houses in this neighborhood were all similar. He didn't know much about architecture, but the boxy design, some with, some without basements, seemed like something from the fifties or sixties. Some of the houses had been renovated, while others allowed to deteriorate. The neglected houses tended to have cars parked in the driveway or on the street, which he interpreted as an indication that the owners were home.

"We need to steal a car," he said.

"You know how to hotwire one?" At his negative response, she continued, "Besides, we get caught, we get put into the system. We know they've infiltrated law enforcement."

"Then how do you suggest we get home?"

"We can't *go* home."

"I meant the city."

She shrugged and then made a face like something had occurred to her. "We need help from someone we can trust, but they're monitoring everyone we know."

"Everyone they know we know."

"Exactly. Who don't they know about?"

They walked in silence for about half a block, and then she turned to him and started to say something, but he stopped her. Over her shoulder, he'd spotted two black SUVs slowly cruising down the cross street. He put his arm around her shoulders and steered her up the walkway of the nearest house, one of the neglected ones. "Act casual. It's them."

They walked right up to the door of the house, and for lack of anything better to do, he rang the bell. A dog inside began to bark furiously; from the high-pitched yapping, he could tell it was a small dog. The door opened a crack and an elderly woman with light cocoa skin and dark freckles peeked out at them.

"Read the door mat!" she snapped.

110

He glanced down. The mat proclaimed that the occupants were broke, knew who they were voting for, and had already found Jesus. He looked back up and smiled at the woman.

"We're not selling anything. We're from the city outreach program and just wondered if you needed help with any chores around the house."

The woman's eyes narrowed in suspicion. "City outreach? Never heard of it." The fact that she hadn't slammed the door in their faces told Dan she wasn't completely convinced that their intentions weren't honorable. Given her age and the condition of the property, she could probably use some help.

"Well, to be honest, it's a program to help young offenders make restitution," he said, deliberately using the word "honest."

"And what offense did you commit?"

Freya spoke up. "We carved our names in a city bench."

"So you're not very smart."

"No ma'am," he replied, taking Freya's hand. "Just in love."

The skepticism on the woman's face faded and the door opened a smidge wider. "How do I know you're telling the truth? What if I let you in and you rob and murder me?"

"Our skillsets are limited to house cleaning and yard work," he said. "We wouldn't have a clue how to rob and murder someone."

That produced a laugh that ended in a bout of coughing. When she recovered, the woman opened the door all the way. She was wearing her bathrobe over a sweatshirt and sweatpants, and she held a matted mop of a dog tucked against her side. "Well, it just so happens I've had the flu this week and the house *has* gotten a bit out of hand."

Chapter Twenty-five

Freya removed the rubber gloves from her hands and draped them over the edge of the kitchen sink. She'd bandaged the gash she'd gotten sliding down the sand dune, but the bandage had gotten soggy and the skin on her fingers was white and wrinkly from hours of being encased in the moist gloves. She'd scrubbed toilets, floors, counters, and inside the refrigerator and stove – not to mention towering piles of festering dishes, pots, and pans. When the old lady, whose name was Mrs. Carson, had said the place had gotten "a bit out of hand," she meant it was filthy in the most disgusting of ways. Not that she really seemed to notice. Freya wasn't sure she'd ever seen so much dust, dirt, mold, and layers of what she could only describe as "crud" covering nearly every surface. And that was *after* she'd gathered the garbage littering the place and tossed it out.

She looked through the kitchen window at the now-tidy backyard. Dan had cleaned, mowed, and weed-wacked, *after* he'd picked up all the dog poop, the quantity of which exposed Mrs. Carson's fib that her lack of cleanliness was due to a week of the flu. More like a year of complete indifference, Freya thought. She'd gone out to put a huge bag of trash in the city can by the side of the house and found that Dan had nearly filled it to the brim with dried-up dog excrement. The smell had literally made her gag.

Mrs. Carson, after having given Freya and Dan a lengthy lecture about the difference between cleaning and reorganizing, and how she would be highly put out if after they were done she couldn't find her scissors or favorite coffee mug, had spent the entire time sitting in a worn-out electric recliner watching soap operas, knitting, and snacking on chips, cookies, and diet soda. Freya suspected she was hard of hearing, because the volume was set to "blast," except during commercials, when the old lady was quick to hit the mute button. While her show was playing, she focused on it to the exclusion of everything going on around her, but when the holovision was muted, she'd gotten into the habit of conversing with Freya about random this and that – whether Freya was in the same room or not. It was annoying for Freya to have to drop whatever she was doing to venture closer to listen to the old lady's ramblings, but it was either that, or shout her responses.

The soap operas tended to play melodramatic music at the end of every scene, so Freya could generally anticipate the commercials. This time when the sound was suddenly cut off, Mrs. Carson stayed silent. Freya looked around the clean kitchen and heaved a sigh of accomplishment but cut it short to grab up the fly swatter and slap it violently down on the counter to end the life of a particularly annoying fly. "Gotcha, you little—"

"Did you say something?" Mrs. Carson called from the living room.

Freya responded reassuringly, "Just killing a fly."

"Oh, I don't know *where* they're coming from."

Mrs. Carson's plaintive cluelessness made Freya look over at Grover the dog and roll her eyes. The little Shih Tzu cocked his head, sending the ponytail holding the fur out of his face flopping to one side. He'd followed Freya everywhere as she cleaned, staring at her adoringly.

Dan came in through the sliding glass door and went to the sink to wash his hands. He brought the smell of the outdoors in with him – grass and pine and the not-unpleasant odor of sweat. Freya moved to stand next to him and said quietly, "Now what?"

His gaze lingered for a moment on the nape of her neck and then he glanced over at the refrigerator. "I gotta eat. Then…I don't know. She's got a car in the garage."

Freya heard the click of claws on the hardwood floor and felt Grover brush against her leg. It hadn't taken long for her to develop a fondness for the little furball. She bent to pet him, feeling guilty that she was even contemplating stealing from his person. Mrs. Carson had told her she was a former nurse who'd been forced into early retirement due to chronic arthritis pain. Spending the afternoon cleaning her house would not make up for stealing her car.

While cleaning, Freya thought about what she and Dan had discussed earlier: who they could trust that Singh's people were unaware of. She'd come to the conclusion that they had only one option – to reach out to her new friends at Temple Grandin High. Sandrew was potentially compromised already considering he'd done that search for her face on the interweb, but if she was careful, she might be able to contact one of the girls through Hologame Club. Jin was the logical choice, not only because she'd displayed the most sympathy towards Freya, but because Freya remembered her Hologame Club screen name, Jin-san.

Dan opened the refrigerator, removed a small container, and popped the corner of the lid open. He sniffed, made a face, and closed it again. The

113

third container to get this treatment passed the sniff test, and he removed the lid entirely before taking a fork Freya had washed out of the dish rack and digging in.

"How's it going in there?" Mrs. Carson asked.

Freya left Dan to his stolen meal and walked into the living room. The pink and blue blanket Mrs. Carson was knitting for premature babies at the local hospital had gotten several inches longer over the course of the afternoon.

"We're done," Freya said cheerfully. "I hate to ask, but would it be okay if I used your holophone? I need to call my parents for a ride home."

Mrs. Carson frowned. "I thought all kids had their own phones these days."

"My mom and dad took it away after I got busted." The lies were rolling more easily off her tongue by the minute.

"Well, alright. It's over there." Mrs. Carson waved one hand in the direction of the dining nook, and with the other hand unmuted the holovision.

Freya already knew where the holophone was; she'd seen it earlier when she'd dusted. From the boxy look of the charging station, she could tell it was an older model, possibly even first generation. She took the phone into the kitchen, knowing she had about ten minutes before the next commercial. She pressed the "on" button and studied the unfamiliar home holo.

"What are you doing?" Dan asked.

"Shhh." She reached into the holo to access the interweb, and then input the address for Hologame Club, ignoring Dan's exaggerated look of skepticism. She opened the app and pinched the "create account" button. As quickly as she could, she input the holomail address Ryan had created for her within the secure XIA network, used "NotACheerSkank" as her new Hologame Club username, and made up a password she would remember. After she submitted the request, she logged in to the XIA holomail. There were a few unopened messages from Ryan, but she didn't have time to read them. She opened the newest message, which was from Hologame Club, and pinched the "verify holomail account" link.

The music from the living room had begun to swell, so she knew she only had a few minutes before the next commercial. She went back to Hologame Club, entered the forums and searched for the screen name "Jin-san." Thankfully, she found it right away – and according to the message board, Jin was currently online.

She input a short message, hoping "Doppelganger S.O.S.," along with her cheerskank screen name would be enough to identify her to Jin.

The response was immediate. "Missed you today. Safe?"

"For now. Need transportation ASAP."

"Road Trip!" Jin responded. "Where r u?"

Freya hesitated and turned to Dan, who'd been watching the exchange, but all he said was, "Careful."

Freya input, "CT" for Connecticut.

"Understood. Bit problematic."

Freya stared into the holo, desperately trying to come up with a way to move forward. Jin and the others had great friendship *potential*, but they hardly knew her, and as things stood, Freya was asking too much of them.

But Jin input, "Can u get to Rye Playland?"

Playland was a seasonal amusement park on the Long Island Sound waterfront in New York, not far from the Connecticut state line. Freya had gone there on a class trip in the fourth grade. She glanced at Dan, who returned her questioning look with a nonplussed one of his own.

Freya input, "Is it open?"

"Not the main park, but Gev's brother Cory works at the ice rink. Ask for him."

Freya had just responded with "Thanks," when Mrs. Carson muted the holovision. Freya added, "Got to go," and signed off. She heard the rumble of the electric motor on Mrs. Carson's recliner, which told her the old lady was on the move. She pasted a smile on her face and left the kitchen to replace the holophone on its charger.

"They're on their way," she said.

Mrs. Carson was shuffling along in her slippers towards the front door, which Freya interpreted as an unsubtle hint that she and Dan weren't welcome to linger, but then Mrs. Carson paused at the coat rack.

"Don't you need me to sign something to prove you were here?" she asked.

Before Freya realized her intention, she reached out and lifted Dan's stolen jacket from the rack. The gun weighed the lightweight jacket down, and even from across the room, Freya could see the pistol grip sticking out of the pocket. Mrs. Carson froze in place, then grasped the gun and pulled it out, dropping the jacket onto the floor. In a move Freya couldn't possibly have anticipated, the old lady swiftly turned, extending her gun arm.

"Thought you could pull a fast one on me, didja?"

Chapter Twenty-six

In the kitchen, Dan heard Mrs. Carson's words and noted the change in tone from neutral to hostile but couldn't fathom what had happened to turn her against them. He set the empty food container into the sink and walked into the living room, only to see Mrs. Carson holding a gun on Freya. As soon as he appeared, she swung her arm around to point the gun at him. He recoiled and lifted his hands into the air.

"That's not a real gun, Ma'am," Freya said.

Dan spotted his jacket on the floor. Mrs. Carson had clearly found the gun in his pocket, which Freya knew all too well was real, but she must be betting on Mrs. Carson not knowing the difference.

"Oh, it's real," Mrs. Carson snapped. "I told you I was a nurse, but not where I worked. Bedford Hills."

Dan had no idea where or what that was, and Freya looked equally unimpressed, so Mrs. Carson clarified, "It was a women's prison. Closed now."

Freya directed a wide-eyed gaze Dan's way. "Did *you* know it was real?"

Dan feigned surprise. "Of course not. How could I?" He turned to Mrs. Carson. "We found it. In the park."

Mrs. Carson's face fell into a bland look of skepticism. "And you just picked it up."

He shrugged. "Yeah. It's cool looking. Should we turn it over to the police?"

Reproof replaced the distrust on Mrs. Carson's face as she lowered her gun arm. "What if someone used this gun to commit a crime and then you came along and got your fingerprints all over it?"

Dan tried to look suitably chastised. "That never occurred to us."

"Kids," Mrs. Carson sighed. "Never thinking about consequences."

Grover growled and then began to bark as he raced to the front door. Someone knocked, and Mrs. Carson went to answer it, holding the gun behind her back and muttering, "Aren't I popular today?"

Dan and Freya moved into the kitchen to listen out of sight. They both smiled when Mrs. Carson practically shouted, "Read the door mat!"

A deep male voice responded. "Police."

"Oh, yeah? Where's your uniform?"

"I'm undercover."

"What do you want?"

"We're investigating a crime in the area, looking for witnesses."

"Since when do undercovers canvass neighborhoods?"

The question was ignored. "Have you seen these two kids?"

Dan grabbed Freya's arm. He was about to drag her to the sliding glass door so they could escape out the back, but Mrs. Carson replied without hesitation. "Nope. What'd they do?"

"That's police business. If you see them, call this number right away."

"Will do."

Dan and Freya stared at each other until they heard the door close, and then peered around the corner at Mrs. Carson. She stood in the middle of the living room with a half-sheet of paper in one hand, gun hand resting at her side.

"Are you going to tell me what kind of trouble you're in?" she asked. "Because if that was a cop, I'm a fire-breathing dragon."

Dan's first thought was that if anyone was the incarnation of a fire-breathing dragon, it was Mrs. Carson. His second thought was for the gun. She was holding hard, cold evidence of their delinquency in her hand, and yet she'd inexplicably protected them.

"You're right. He wasn't a cop," Freya said, voice cracking, "but even if we could tell you what's going on, you wouldn't believe us."

"You know," Mrs. Carson replied, "I've been around the block. Several times. In my line of work, I met all kinds. Most of the inmates at Bedford Hills deserved to be there, but there were a few who didn't. Neither of you strike me as criminals, but I can't help you if I don't know what you've gotten yourselves into."

Dan stepped tentatively into the living room. "He wanted to kill us."

"*Kill* you?" Mrs. Carson laughed. "What on earth did you do?"

"Nothing," Freya said.

Mrs. Carson's mirth faded fast. "Not a thing? What about this?" She lifted the gun. "Still sticking with the 'we found it' story?"

"We did find it, but you're right, we knew it was real," Dan said. "We took it to protect ourselves."

"Shouldn't your parents be protecting you? You said they were on their way."

Freya glanced away from Mrs. Carson's penetrating stare. "They're not."

"You runaways?"

"Kind of," Dan said. "I mean, we're running away from certain death."

"Oh, for crying out loud. Seriously? I'm this close to calling the *actual* police."

"Please don't," Freya said. "The truth is…our parents are in protective custody, because we know something – something that a very rich and powerful person doesn't want anyone to know, and he sent his men to eliminate us. Which puts you in danger, too, unless you let us go before they find out we were here. If you call the police, we're dead for sure."

"Isn't that an episode from, I don't know, every crime show ever?" Mrs. Carson asked.

Freya looked taken aback. "That fake cop on your porch was real. These guys don't mess around. They have drones, and nanotech, and big guns. They've infiltrated law enforcement and have access to street cameras and all kinds of other stuff. They killed everyone involved except me and my mom. Dan got dragged into it without knowing what he was getting into. And we're scared to death."

"How did you end up on my doorstep?"

"Randomly," Dan said. "We saw them coming and went to the nearest house."

"Lucky me."

"Look, we're really sorry," Freya said. "We panicked. We weren't thinking how this might affect you. We just needed a place to hide."

Mrs. Carson stared at Freya for a long moment, and then sighed heavily and looked down at the sheet of paper in her hand.

"Can we see that?" Dan asked.

Mrs. Carson held it out. Dan reached out to take it, warily eyeing the gun. He and Freya examined the grainy side-by-side photos taken from somewhere above them. Their faces had been closely cropped, but even without the benefit of a background to give him a sense of place, he knew from the lighting and the dirt on their faces that the shots had been taken this morning on the beach after the grenade went off. The text on the paper had their names and descriptions, and the words, "Armed and dangerous. Do not attempt to detain," followed by a phone number to call.

"These must have been taken before the XIA took out their drone," Freya said quietly.

Mrs. Carson, who Dan would have sworn was deaf as all get out, exclaimed, "The XIA? Are you kidding me? This has something to do with xenofreaks?"

Her outrage told him she wasn't exactly fond of xenos.

"Not really," Freya said. "It has to with the medical benefits of xenografts."

Mrs. Carson pondered that for a moment. "Because xenos hardly ever get sick? Which was a well-known but unofficial fact at the prison, and I worked in the medical ward, so I should know. Place was crawling with xenos, but I only saw them for injuries."

"I'd tell you more, not that I know the whole story, but you've been so nice." Freya took an earnest step towards her. "You really are in danger." She gestured to the gun. "Let us go."

"Go where?"

"I contacted a friend when I used your holophone. We're going to meet up with someone."

"If what you're saying is true, you walk out that door, odds are they'll catch you. I'm not sure I want that on my conscience." Mrs. Carson shuffled over to the coat rack, kicked off her slippers and stepped into a scuffed pair of loafers.

"We got this far," Dan said. He wasn't sure why Mrs. Carson took off her bathrobe, tossed it onto her chair, and then switched the gun from one hand to the other as she tugged a black sweater peppered with dog hair over her sweatshirt. She topped the ensemble off by covering her mussed hair with a knitted black beanie.

"There're blankets in the hall closet," she said, looking at Freya. "On the second shelf, there's a hideous green and orange quilt my former mother-in-law made. Will you get it for me, dear?"

Freya did as she asked, but when she brought it back into the living room and tried to hand it to Mrs. Carson, the old woman said, "Oh, that's for you. You'll need something to cover you in the back seat of my car."

Chapter Twenty-seven

The car was a clunky old Cadillac with a gasoline engine, but it had once been considered a luxury vehicle, as evidenced by the roomy, leather-upholstered back seat. Not that the seat itself was visible under what appeared to be decades of garbage layered like decaying leaves on a forest floor. While Mrs. Carson buckled Grover into his doggy restraining strap in the passenger seat, Freya and Dan began shoving the trash into bags. It took them several minutes to remove the bulk of it, and then, in a scenario reminiscent of the previous evening's boat adventure, they lay down on the seat and covered themselves with the quilt.

Freya had heard the term "spooning" before but hadn't really considered the intimacy of the position. She lay curled up on the edge of the seat in front of Dan, head resting on one of his arms while his other arm loosely embraced her. The enforced closeness added a new component to the fear she always felt in his company. When Mrs. Carson pulled the car out of the garage, the chassis bounced enthusiastically down the driveway, prompting Dan to tighten his hold against the jostling. The unintended embrace sparked a not entirely unwelcome sensation throughout Freya's midsection, like weakness and need rolled into one. Her uneasiness of him began to recede, crowded out by these new feelings. She felt her face flush when she imagined turning indolently towards him to entangle her limbs with his.

The car ride seemed long and arduous. Her world constricted to a pinpoint of awareness as she struggled to appear unaffected by his proximity, afraid her breathing would give her away every time her mind conjured up a fresh batch of images to go along with her carnal thoughts. The worst part was not knowing whether he was similarly affected. She couldn't trust her instincts. When he shifted his hips, was it discomfort from their cramped position, or was he trying to keep the evidence of his own arousal hidden from her? She honestly didn't know and wasn't about to risk exposing her raw emotions to find out.

There wasn't much to distract herself with, since her field of view under the quilt was limited to the floor of the car, but she'd counted two dollars and twelve cents in change, and an astonishing thirty-six dropped French fries in various stages of desiccation. Thankfully, Mrs. Carson left no silence unfilled, and Freya found her prattle occasionally diverting. From the sound of it, Mrs. Carson was attempting to speak without moving her lips in case anyone was watching, which was a constant source of amusement to Freya given that everyone talked on their dash cams while driving anyway. When Mrs. Carson finally announced that they were nearly there, Freya's relief was profound.

"I don't want to alarm you," Mrs. Carson said a few minutes later, "but there's been a car behind us for quite some time. I'm about to hit the exit, so we'll see what he does."

"What kind of car?" Dan asked.

"Black SUV. Looks like just the driver."

Dan muttered a few choice expletives. Mrs. Carson went into a long turn, and then confirmed the worst. "He's still behind us. What should I do?"

"Go someplace well populated," Freya said.

"Okay, I—*Hey!* What the...?" Mrs. Carson braked, turned sharply, accelerated briefly and then braked so suddenly that Freya slid off the seat onto the floor.

"Sorry, kids," Mrs. Carson said once they'd come to a stop. "He forced us onto a side road. This is it. Stay hidden. I'll take care of it."

Freya stayed on the floor but made sure the quilt was still covering her. She heard the power window motor and the chirping of birds from outside.

"Have you lost your mind?" Mrs. Carson cried.

"Get out of the car." It was the same voice deep voice from earlier. Grover barked, and then growled low and long.

"I will *not*," Mrs. Carson said. "You're that cop that came to my door. What precinct are you from? Because last time I checked, the police use the lights on their cruisers to pull people over, instead of forcing them off the road."

There was a sound like the man slammed his hand forcefully against the roof of the car. "You lied to me, old lady. Your neighbor said she saw those kids go into your house."

"Which neighbor?" Mrs. Carson demanded. "Because if it was that drunk Nadine Klein across the street, then you've been had. She's hated me since the summer of '18, when she claimed her stupid dog ran out into the street and got hit because my son set off a string of firecrackers. Seven hundred dollars in vet bills she thinks I owe just because her mutt couldn't handle a little noise."

"What's under that blanket back there?"

"None of your beeswax, that's what. Show me your identification. I know my rights."

"You have the right to remain silent and do as you're told."

Mrs. Carson dropped the indignant tone. "A real cop wouldn't hesitate to properly identify himself."

"Those kids been telling you stories?"

"I asked to see your badge." Mrs. Carson's voice had lowered considerably, and she sounded almost resigned.

Her seeming acquiescence only emboldened the man, who stated coldly, "My *badge* has a clip of bullets in it." He laughed shortly and without humor. "You know what? I don't even know why I'm talking to you. You're just expendable meat. What the Clan refers to as collateral dam—"

A deafening blast cut him off, immediately followed by a second one. Terrified, Freya's instinct was to run rather than be a sitting duck, but to her utter amazement Mrs. Carson spoke. "He was reaching for his gun. You kids'll need to get him off the road. Hurry before someone drives by."

Dan threw the quilt aside and without a word, exited the car. Freya, shocked as speechless as he was, followed more slowly. Mrs. Carson stayed put, a defensive yet resolute look on her face.

Outside, fresh country air cleared the acrid odor of gunpowder from Freya's nostrils. The man on the ground wasn't as big as his deep voice had suggested. The front of his shirt was soaked bright red, and from his position, he must have rocked back on his heels and fallen straight and stiff onto his back, a surprised look frozen on his face. His jacket was open, revealing a shoulder holster and gun. There was no badge in evidence.

"Don't touch anything that will leave a print!" Mrs. Carson advised through the open window. "Don't step in the blood or get any on yourselves, and for God's sake, don't barf. You don't want to leave any DNA."

Freya had been suppressing the urge to vomit since she'd gotten a glimpse of the man's brown eyes staring unseeing up at the sky. Mrs. Carson's instructions only strengthened that urge, but she forced herself to join Dan near the dead man's head. A dozen thoughts and feelings jostled for precedence, but "avoid detection" won out. Her only objective as she grasped the man's limp left arm was to hide the evidence of Mrs. Carson's crime as quickly as possible. They tugged the corpse around the front of the car and onto the side of the road. Once they'd deposited it in the middle of a tall patch of weeds, Dan crouched down, pulled his sleeves down to cover his hands, and gingerly removed the man's gun, wallet, and keys.

"I didn't think shit could *get* any more real," he said.

"I know," she replied weakly.

He didn't wait for Mrs. Carson to bark out further instructions. He trotted to the black SUV, which the dead man had hastily parked sticking partway into the road, and with his hands still covered by his sleeves, opened the driver's side door. Freya watched numbly as he drove a short distance onto the shoulder. As soon as he got out, Mrs. Carson called, "Get in the car!"

Freya and Dan scrambled into the back seat, and when the door slammed behind them Mrs. Carson peeled out so fast the Caddy's bald tires squealed on the tarmac.

Chapter Twenty-eight

Dan would have understood if Mrs. Carson had gone all tight-lipped for the rest of the trip, but she didn't. If anything, she became more talkative.

"So many women would have hesitated," she said, her words coming out in a stilted monotone. "Would have waited to be very, very sure the danger was real before they pulled the trigger. At the prison we called those women victims. The survivors are the ones who don't second-guess their intuition. This one inmate, Anita was her name, had an abusive husband. At first, he told her if she reported him, he was going to kill her, but eventually, he just flat out told her he'd kill her someday. That threat was always empty…until the day it wasn't. She knew deep down that day would come; had been mentally preparing for it for years. She'd memorized every potential weapon in the house. Not just knives, but lamps, vases, cords on appliances. She'd fantasized constantly about how to use them to protect herself, so no matter where the attack came from, she'd have some form of self-defense."

"What happened to her?" Freya asked.

"Beat him to a pulp with a bookend. Of course with all her preparedness, you'd think she would have recorded him making threats or something, but no. She had zero evidence to support her testimony and of course the scumbag's lawyer presented him in court as a model citizen." She paused for a moment. "When push comes to shove, you kids gonna hang me out to dry?"

"Of course not. You saved us back there." Dan grasped the back of her seat but stopped short of offering physical comfort. She wasn't the kind of person you patted on the shoulder. "You probably shouldn't go home. In fact, you might want to ditch the car. They're gonna be looking for it."

"I was just thinking that. I'll go straight to the bus station. I'm due for a visit with my sister in Jersey anyway." Mrs. Carson smiled, but the corners of her mouth drooped almost immediately.

"Keep the gun, though," Dan said. "For protection. I've got his gun."

She nodded. "Not keen on carrying the murder weapon around, but I'll dispose of it once I get to my sister's place."

"My cousin works for the XIA," Freya said. "Once things die down, he'll be in touch."

Mrs. Carson made a left turn into a huge, mostly empty parking lot. The Playland complex sprawled along the shore of the bay. She put the car into park with the engine running, and then twisted in her seat, but she couldn't quite make eye contact. "I'm a foolish old woman who took a leap of faith trusting you kids, and now I'm a killer because of it. Just so you know, that was *not* on my bucket list."

Freya made a sound like a stifled sob and practically hurled herself across the back of the seat into Mrs. Carson's arms. Dan looked out the window, trying to keep his emotions at bay. Freya kept repeating how sorry she was, and Mrs. Carson said, "Me, too, honey. Me, too."

After a few minutes, Dan put a hand on Freya's back. "We should go."

She pulled away and stared at Mrs. Carson with haunted eyes. "*Thank you.*"

"You stay safe," Mrs. Carson replied.

"You, too."

Dan reached for the door handle, but Mrs. Carson said, "Wait!" She took her black beanie off and held it out to Freya. "Dan here has a hood, but you should cover your hair. Oh, and hold on." She opened the glove compartment and riffled through the items inside. "These'll do," she said, handing Freya a pair of large, old-fashioned sunglasses.

"Thanks." Freya put the hat and glasses on and forced a grin. "How do I look?"

Mrs. Carson's dry sense of humor reasserted itself briefly. "It's an improvement. You got cash? Because admission isn't free."

"Yeah, we're good, thanks." Dan hadn't opened the dead man's wallet, but he'd seen the telltale edges of some bills sticking out.

He and Freya got out of the car and waved as Mrs. Carson drove away.

"I hope she'll be alright," Freya said.

"She's a tough old bird." He spotted a trash can near the park entrance. "Come on."

The trash can was full to overflowing. He picked out a grease-stained fast food bag resting on top and opened it. Inside, he found what he was looking for: several unused napkins among the wadded-up burger wrappers. Using one of the napkins, he took the dead man's keys out of his pocket and dropped them into the bag. Then he did the same with the dead man's wallet, but not before removing the cash. He stuffed the fast food bag back into the trash can far enough that it wouldn't fall out, and then brushed his hands down the front of his shorts. He doubted any amount of wiping would remove the sense of horror and guilt at what he'd done.

"How much is there?" Freya asked.

"Eighty bucks. Let's go."

There weren't many people around when they entered the park, but he kept his voice low just in case. "How are we supposed to find this guy?"

"Ask someone, I guess. And we better hurry. If they aren't already tracking us," she waved a hand to broadly indicate the security cameras on every building, "then they will be as soon as their guy doesn't check in, or whatever. We probably don't have much time."

He nodded and increased his pace to keep up with her as she strode towards the art deco building housing the ice rink. The gun he'd tucked into the small of his back shifted, so he shoved his hands in the pockets of his shorts to tighten the elastic waistband. It was noisy inside the huge old building, filled with the echoing voices of children. In the lobby, Freya took off the sunglasses, but kept her head down. A smiling young woman sat at a table decorated with helium balloons that read, "Happy Birthday!"

"You here for one of the parties?" she asked.

Dan shook his head.

He and Freya wove their way through excited kids bundled up against the cold. On the ice, a skater wearing a bear costume was entertaining a group of children by pretending he couldn't skate. Every time he fell, arms and legs akimbo, peals of laughter rang out.

"We shouldn't be here," Freya said.

He knew what she meant. It was tempting to think a crowd was a good place to hide, but the men chasing them might not hesitate to shoot anyway. Dan wouldn't be able to live with himself if even one of these innocent kids got hurt.

"Yeah, I think we need a plan B."

They turned back towards the entrance just in time to see two men enter. There were quite a few dads in the crowd, but these guys were dressed in camo like soldiers of fortune and didn't blend in at all. They stood by the entrance and scanned the area, clearly looking for someone. Goose bumps popped up all over Dan's body from the cold – or maybe, if he was being

126

honest with himself, from fear. Freya grabbed his arm and pulled him down to sit next to her on the nearest bench. She bent over like she was removing her shoes.

"How did they find us so fast?" she whispered.

"It's got to be the nanotech. We didn't wash it all off. As soon as we got out of Mrs. Carson's car, the sun activated it and they got a ping or something. And I bet they were already in the area because the guy who was following us called for backup."

He watched the men out of the corner of his eye. Thankfully, they headed in the opposite direction, and even the obliviously frenzied children got out of their way like water parting at the prow of a boat.

Dan looked around for the telltale red glow of an exit sign. The employee in the bear costume skated over to the dasher board directly in front of them.

"Hey!" The voice coming out of the big round bear head was muffled. "You Gev's friends?"

The bear must have correctly interpreted the desperation on their faces, because he dug a toe pick into the ice and sprang through the opening in the dasher boards. "Let's go. Chop, chop!" He herded them into a back room, shut the door, and removed his head. His cheeks and nose were ruddy from the cold, but his short, dark blond hair was wet with sweat.

"I'm Cory." His grin was lopsided, as if only one side of his face worked properly. He sat and swiftly removed his skates. "Gev says you guys are in trouble. What kind of trouble?"

"The life or death kind," Dan said.

Cory unzipped the front of his costume and stripped it off. "Those scary dudes lookin' for you?" He turned to Freya, but before she could respond, he said, "Damn. Gev said you were pretty, but she didn't say you were *gorgeous*."

Dan frowned in irritation, but bit back the retort on the tip of his tongue. If the price of Cory's help was ignoring his flirtation attempts, he would gladly pay it.

"Thanks," Freya said, sounding anything but thankful, "but I'm gonna make a gorgeous corpse if we don't get out of here."

"I got you covered." Cory tossed the bear head to Dan, who barely reacted fast enough to catch it, but instantly figured out what he had in mind.

"No way," he said. "This isn't a sitcom. I'm not wearing it."

Cory laughed. "Just messin' with you. My van's parked nearby."

He shoved his feet into a pair of canvas shoes and reached for the doorknob. "This way."

Chapter Twenty-nine

Cory poked his head out the door, looked in the direction of the rink, and then ushered them into the corridor. Freya was too stressed to notice much about their surroundings as he led them through the old building and out a back exit. He strode confidently into the late afternoon sunshine and had gone several yards when he realized they weren't following him. He turned. "What's wrong?"

"We need to stay out of the sun," she said.

"How come? You vampires?"

"Of course not. We got covered with solar-activated nanotech. Plus, they've got drones and can access security cameras. I know you probably think we're crazy paranoid, but–"

"Not my first mechanical bull ride," he replied. "Wait here."

Freya skulked in the shadows with Dan until Cory returned driving a dirty white cargo van. The back door slid open automatically, and they climbed in. The inside had been amateurly outfitted as a tiny house, about as small as their cabin on Maddy Singh's yacht, but significantly less glamorous. There was a narrow walking space down the center of the cargo area, splitting it into two halves. On one side, white laminate cupboards and shelving had been mounted to the van wall, and on the other side, a padded shelf with storage underneath served as both seating and bed. The pad was covered with a poorly folded comforter, as if Cory had hastily tidied the place only minutes ago. Dan sat on it, and she tentatively joined him, nose wrinkled against the strong odor of unwashed bedding.

"Welcome to mi casa," Cory said from the driver's seat. He drove a short distance, parked the van, and then rotated his seat so he was facing them. "There's a privacy curtain so no one can see in through the front windows, snacks and soda in the upper cupboard, and if you need it, there's a bucket in the lower one, if you get my drift. You'll have to hide here till my shift's over, but then I can drive you into the city."

128

"How long?" Dan asked.

"Three more hours. I'll leave the keys in the ignition in case it gets too hot in here. Tank's full, but the air conditioner'll suck it dry, so don't use it if you can possibly help it. Sorry, but I gotta jet." His uneven grin made another appearance. "My little fanbase'll be wondering where Clumsy Bear went."

"Cory," Freya said.

He directed a questioning look her way, and she said, "Thanks."

"For friends of my little sister? Anything."

As soon as he exited the van, Dan jumped up to check that the doors were locked, and then pulled the curtain, which plunged them into near darkness. While her eyes adjusted, she listened to him explore the cupboards, until she heard the telltale crinkle of a plastic bag.

"Want some chips?" he asked.

"No thanks."

He tore the bag open, muttering, "It reeks in here."

She looked down at the comforter. "He probably can't get to a laundromat as often as he should."

"Yeah, well, I'm not looking forward to inhaling Cory funk for the next three hours."

"Doesn't smell any worse than the fishing boat."

"Is that supposed to be an endorsement?"

"No, but...gift horse."

Dan had shoved several chips into his mouth, but he lifted his eyebrows in agreement. He set the chips down and resumed his hunting expedition, opening every cupboard and pawing through the contents. When he knelt to look under the bed shelf, she moved her legs out of the way, conscious of the close quarters.

"Aha!" he said, removing a folded blanket and holding it to his nose. "Not fresh out of the dryer, but at least it isn't..." he made a disgusted face.

They stuffed the comforter and pillow into the cupboard, and then spread the blanket out over the shelf. Dan took the gun from his waistband and set it on top of one of the cupboards before he sat down. Freya took off Mrs. Carson's beanie and the sunglasses and then sat next to him. The silence was broken only by the sound of Dan crunching chips.

Out of the blue, he said, "I'm gonna get fat."

She snorted. "But eating still helps, right? Suppress the weird urges?"

"Enough for me to handle them. How's your hand?"

"Could use a new bandage."

"Let me see." He reached out, but she pulled her hand away.

"It's fine. I'm just...tired. I'm going to try to take a nap, okay?"

She stretched out on the shelf with her back to the wall of the van, head resting on her arm.

He stood and took his jacket off, rolling it up and offering it to her as a pillow. There was nowhere for him to sit other than the floor, so she said, "Lay down with me."

If he was surprised at the invitation, it didn't show on his face. Freya was probably more surprised at herself. He joined her, moving slowly and deliberately, and she couldn't tell if it was because he was reluctant, or was being careful not to jostle her. He lay down on his side facing away from her, just like they had in Mrs. Carson's car, except their positions were reversed.

Freya closed her eyes and tried to relax. For some reason, she found herself envisioning the cool, damp cavern at the beach. She tried to conjure the sense of comfort it had given her – before all hell broke loose, that is. She almost managed to clear her mind of negative thoughts – fear, anger, pain – but once again, Dan's nearness began to unravel her concentration. She opened her eyes and stared at the back of his neck. His head moved, like he'd asked himself an internal question and answered it with a tiny, negative headshake.

"What?" she asked quietly.

"I can't." He started to sit up, but she put a hand on his shoulder. With no intention of doing so, she slid her hand down his arm and then raised it again, up and under his shirt sleeve until her fingers grazed his xenograft.

Quite suddenly, but not unexpectedly, he rolled towards her. He stared into her eyes, and Freya knew her face mirrored his look of confused longing. His hand found her lower back and he gently dug his fingernails into the fur of her graft, sending a wave of pleasurable chill bumps radiating outward. She let out a breath she didn't realize she'd been holding right before he kissed her.

Chapter Thirty

Dan's misgivings about his own motivation, both his conscious intentions toward Freya and the unconscious urges he'd been suffering through, melted away when his mouth found hers. He was briefly gratified that her response seemed to match his in intensity, but all rational thought was quickly smothered under an avalanche of fervent need. His senses became acutely attuned as he explored the contrasting softness and firmness of her body: the way she wriggled under his boldly wandering hands; her gasps of pleasure; his glimpses of her face, eyes closed, mouth ardently slack, brows scrunched together; but especially the scent rising from her fevered skin – he savored each inhalation like an addictive drug.

He was so enthralled with her, all thought of his xenograft and its aggressive influence over him disappeared. He lightly dragged his fingertips along the skin of her back, up under her shirt to her bra. When he began fumbling with the hooks, however, she pulled away, a regretful look on her face. For a moment – just an instant, really, that he immediately quashed – he wasn't sure he would be able to stop. He took a deep breath and rolled onto his back as his self-control reasserted itself.

"You okay?" she asked softly.

With a gleefully abashed grin, he turned his head to look at her. "I'm great. You?"

She returned his smile. "Yeah."

"Maybe we should–"

Forceful banging on the back of the van cut him off and he froze. Several tense seconds passed with no further noise from outside.

"If it was Cory, he'd say something," Freya whispered.

"Are we in a no parking zone?"

"Hope not."

He sat up. "I'm getting the gun just in case."

131

He reached for it, but before he could close his fingers around the grip, the van rocked as someone shattered one of the windows in the cab. A hissing noise preceded the appearance of white smoke curling around the edges of the privacy curtain. His eyes began to sting, his nose burned, and a choking sensation engulfed his throat. He knew it was tear gas, and he also knew it was intended to force them out of the van, where they'd be easily picked off. He tried to hold his breath, but when he couldn't, it felt like his lungs had been filled with cement. Despite knowing what was in store for them outside, he clawed blindly at the door handle. As the door slid open, Freya, most likely as desperate as he, pushed him from behind.

They stumbled out onto the tarmac and lurched away from the van. Something struck him on the shoulder, and he fell. He rolled onto his back, hands held up defensively. Through eyes streaming with tears, he saw a man standing over him, gun aimed at his face. He blinked, and the man's face came briefly into focus. The last thing Dan expected was to recognize him.

He heard Freya let out a garbled scream, and another man said, "I got her. Do it!"

Dan braced for the shot, but instead, Cerberus pulled his gun arm back and struck him in the face.

. . .

"Hey!"

Someone was shaking his shoulder.

"Dude, wake up!"

Dan opened his eyes. They felt swollen, and his eyelashes were crusted together. It was dark and he was lying on something hard. He recoiled from the shadowy figure looming over him, until he recognized the voice.

"Cory?"

"You okay? Where's Freya?"

Freya? Dan turned his head to the side. The van door was open, all trace of tear gas gone.

"They took her." He put his hands over his face and gingerly rubbed his stinging eyes. He wanted to get up, but the pounding in his head suggested that wasn't an option quite yet.

"Oh, man, your face is covered in blood. Looks like your nose is broken."

Dan sniffed and swallowed congealed blood, which turned his stomach. He rolled onto his side and gagged.

Cory disappeared from view for a few minutes while Dan lay on the ground trying to pull himself together. He heard the van door close, and then Cory reappeared, putting a wet cloth to Dan's face. Dan reached up to take it, muttering, "Thanks."

After a few more minutes holding the cool cloth to his eyes, Dan forced himself up onto one of his elbows. "What time is it?"

"A little after eight. How long you been layin' here?"

"Couple hours, I guess." Dan sat up, expecting the wave of dizziness that followed.

"And nobody helped you?" Cory said. "I hate people. We gotta get you to the hospital."

"No. No way." Dan struggled to his feet, grateful for Cory's steadying hand on his arm. "We need to find Freya."

"You know where they took her?"

Dan shook his head, but immediately regretted it.

"Alright, well, best to get movin' and figure out where we're goin' when we're on the road. Come on." Cory helped Dan to the passenger side of the van, opened the door, and brushed glass shards from the seat before easing him into it and shutting the door.

He gave the same treatment to the driver's seat before he climbed in and started the engine. Frowning at the broken window, he said, "Lucky it's not cold out."

Dan flipped down the sun visor and looked into the little mirror on the backside. He wiped the worst of the blood from his face, silently agreeing with Cory that his nose was probably broken. "You got any aspirin?"

"In the glove compartment, but it's a bit stronger than aspirin."

Dan found a prescription bottle with a woman's name on the label. He didn't ask, nor did he care where Cory had gotten it. He dumped two pills into his palm.

Cory gestured to a fast food cup resting in the cup holder. "Just melted ice from yesterday's soda, but it'll do."

"Thanks," Dan replied. "You got a phone?"

"Sorry, man. Clumsy Bear doesn't make enough. I got a burner, but I'm out of time."

"Maybe we can stop somewhere. I need to call the XIA."

"The *what*? Why?"

"Long story. Where're we going?"

"The original plan was to drive you to New York. Thought maybe that'd be a good start."

Dan swallowed the pills, sucking down all of the stale water in the cup. Then he sighed and laid his aching head against the head rest. As soon as did, a flash of memory hit him.

"Cerberus," he said.

"What?"

"My friend Wade. His dad's xeno name is Cerberus. He's the one who hit me."

"Seriously? So who are these guys? Why are they after you?"

Dan figured Cory was already knee deep into it, so it couldn't hurt to brief him. After he'd given him a bare-bones explanation, Cory said, "You didn't know this Cerberus guy was part of it?"

"No, but I knew he was in a gang called the Clan." Ryan had identified the graft on that mercenary's arm back at the beach as a spotted hyena, so the Clan was clearly involved.

"Oh, I heard of them. What's it…hyenas or something? Also known as The Bitches?"

Dan nodded, noting that his head pain had significantly decreased. The pills were kicking in.

"Yeah," he said. "The gang's run by women, just like real hyenas."

"Kinky," Cory said.

"I got the impression Wade was embarrassed, but he never talked about it much. I guess I should be grateful it was Cerberus. Anyone else would have shot me."

"You think Freya's okay?"

"If she's still alive, it won't be for long." Dan was slurring some of his words and having a hard time thinking. "They're probably setting something up to look like an accident as we speak." Just the thought of it made him want to cry. He'd done a lousy job protecting her.

"You should put your seat back. Maybe catch a few z's."

Dan was too woozy to even reply. He reached his hand around and pulled the lever to lower the seat. It was the last thing he remembered before dozing off.

Chapter Thirty-one

One of the men who'd kidnapped Freya sat next to her in the back seat while the other drove the SUV a short way and then stopped to pick someone up. Freya wasn't certain, but she thought the short-haired woman who climbed into the passenger seat was the same one who'd been in charge back at the beach. The one who'd ordered her subordinate to toss the grenade into the cave.

"Serb," the woman said. "You take care of the boy?"

"Yes, Matron," said the man sitting next to Freya, but she caught an exchange of glances in the rear-view mirror between Serb and the driver – and noticed the driver's quickly-hidden look of skepticism. It was a small, subtle thing, but she clung to it. If "take care of" meant what she thought it did, then Serb had been ordered to kill Dan. Back at the van, everything had happened so fast, and the tear gas had all but blinded her, but there'd been nothing wrong with her hearing. After the driver had grabbed her, he'd clamped a hand over her mouth and yelled, "I got her. Do it!" She'd heard a grunt and a thud, like a body hitting the ground. No gunshots, not that Serb couldn't have used a quieter method of murdering Dan…but the driver's skeptical look…it might mean that Serb hadn't followed through. She made a mental note that just *maybe* the woman didn't have complete control of her underlings. If Serb was sympathetic, Freya might be able to take advantage of that.

The driver took the onramp to the interstate and kept to the speed limit. Freya had watched enough holovision to know that her captors not blindfolding her was a bad sign. Not that she had any delusions about her fate. Her only hope was to escape, but from the hypervigilance of her captors, she wasn't likely to get an opportunity. They drove, according to the holoclock on the dash, for almost two hours, and the electrigas gauge indicated they had over a hundred miles left before they'd need to recharge and refuel. Best case scenario, they'd have to stop for food or to use the restroom, but Freya had already resigned herself to the worst-case scenario – that they'd drive straight through to their destination.

At first, she figured they'd take her someplace remote where no one would ever find her body, but then when the New York skyline came into view, she decided they were sticking to the "accidental death" formula that had worked so well on all the others. Before this, Freya thought she knew what fear felt like, but nothing brought that visceral emotion into sharper focus than the anticipation of her imminent demise. Her thoughts skittered between memories of her life – happy times with family and friends - and formulating desperate plans of action – like leaping out of the moving vehicle or wresting the sidearm away from Serb and shooting the others with it.

"May I have a drink of water?" she asked him.

"No." He didn't even turn his head. So much for sympathy.

She looked out the window, staring past light reflections on the glass to the one star visible in the sky. *Probably not even a star*, she thought bleakly. *Can't wish on a planet or airplane.*

It was Thursday evening, and traffic in the city was as light as it ever got. As they drove through Brooklyn, Freya stared in the general direction of Mouse's apartment even though she knew her mother was in a safe house somewhere. Tears that she could no longer hold back began to stream down her face.

Serb reached into the pocket on the back of the driver's seat and pulled out a tissue. When he held it out to her, she thought it was another sign that he wasn't completely insensitive until he muttered, "Quitcher sniffling."

Freya was mildly surprised when they crossed the bridge onto Staten Island. She'd only been there a few times but had learned its basic history in school. The thing that had struck her most about the island at the time was the number of parks and waterways with the word "kill" in their name. She knew it was an old Dutch word meaning "river," but as they approached Arthur Kill on the west side of the island, its meaning took on new significance.

The driver turned onto a street and drove to a sprawling, four-story office complex, ignoring several signs that proclaimed the area as dangerous. The building was completely dark, lit only from the exterior by streetlights. He stopped at the entrance to let Freya, Matron, and Serb out. Matron unlocked the main door and Freya was marched inside straight to a stairwell. As she climbed up by the light of Serb's holophone, she contemplated whether life-after-death existed, and for the first time truly understood the enormous appeal of the concept.

136

Chapter Thirty-two

Dan opened his eyes and reflexively turned his head away from the shaft of white sunshine glaring in through the van window. He raised a hand to rub his face and immediately wished he hadn't as his fingers encountered his swollen, painful nose. The prior evening's memories rushed in.

Freya.

"Cory?" he called, thinking Gev's brother was asleep in the back. There was no response, so he opened the door and stumbled out onto the sidewalk in front of an unfamiliar apartment complex. His nose was completely blocked, but he took a deep breath of fresh air through his mouth, hoping it would clear his head. As he stood there foggily sorting through his options, he heard voices and turned to see Cory with his sister Gev, as well her whole gang of friends. Everyone but Cory was carrying a backpack; they were clearly headed to school.

"You look like crap," Sandrew said.

"Thanks," Dan muttered. He looked at Cory. "Did you call?"

"The XIA? Tried to." He shrugged. "No one answered the main line and the hotline was just for leaving messages."

"Please tell me you didn't."

"Think I'm stupid?"

Dan regarded him for a moment. Cory had an innocent face and his persona was everyman's goofball, but there was real intelligence behind his eyes – and more importantly, shrewdness.

"No," Dan said. "So, do we know *anything*?"

"Not really."

Cory started to say something else, but Jin interrupted with, "We got a plan, though."

"What?" Dan snapped. "No. No harebrained schemes. I need to get hold of the XIA. Freya's cousin–"

Cindy snorted. "What does harebrained even mean?"

137

"I know, right?" Sandrew said.

"We need to stay on topic." Gev looked at Dan, lips puckered disapprovingly. "Did we or did we not save your bacon last night?"

Cindy opened her mouth but closed it again when Gev made an "eh" sound like she was correcting a dog. Probably, Dan thought, to stop Cindy from asking what "save your bacon" was supposed to mean.

He glanced at Cory. "Yeah. Seriously…thanks."

"Okay, then," Gev continued. "Cory told us about your insane adventure, and we think your best bet is to talk with Wade."

Dan's head went back as he considered it. "That's a good idea."

Every one of them rolled their eyes as if they'd synchronized their reaction.

"We do come up with those once in a while," Kaye said.

Cory gestured to the van. "Pile in, peoples."

It turned out they were only a few blocks from Temple Grandin High. Cory double-parked to let everyone out.

"This is where I get off," he said. "Clumsy Bear works in a couple hours."

Dan thanked him again before stalking off across the grass straight for Wade, who was standing in his usual spot at the top of the mound. Wade watched him come with narrowed eyes.

Dan had every intention of punching him in his ugly face, but suddenly Bass was there, heading him off.

"Whoa! What happened to *you*?" he exclaimed. "Your mom was off the rails last night when you didn't come home."

"Not now," Dan said, pushing past his friend.

Bass grabbed his arm in a surprisingly aggressive move. "Don't do it. There were shots fired, mistakes made…he didn't leave you there on purpose."

Dan paused just long enough to glance at Bass with a tight smile. "Yeah, he did. Now let go."

Bass released his grip and stepped to the side; hands held up in defeat.

Dan was ten feet away when Wade called out, "Really? You wanna go at it with me? Cause I'll take you on any day and twice on Sunday."

Most of the students in the vicinity began to melt away, but a few took out their holophones to catch the action. Dan barely noticed. His sole focus was Wade. When he got within striking distance, he held back with a monumental effort, fists clenched at his side.

"Where is she?" he snarled.

138

Wade crossed his arms. "Who?" he asked, but something about his defensiveness told Dan he already knew.

"Freya."

"How should I know?" Wade looked annoyed. "You were with her."

"Yeah, up until your dad kidnapped her."

Wade wasn't a good enough actor to fake his look of incredulous surprise. He laughed, and Dan only stopped himself from responding with a right hook to the jaw because he didn't want it to look like a sucker punch.

"My *dad*," Wade started to say through clenched teeth, but then he hesitated and finished in a more resigned tone, "only does what he's told."

The adrenaline that had propelled Dan across the campus began to fade. "Nah," he said. "He was *told* to kill me, but he did this instead." He gestured to his face.

"He does good work," Wade responded, and Dan knew it was his twisted way of bringing the conversation around to something more rational.

"Where is he?"

Wade shook his head like he had no idea, but then said, "Probably in the killzone."

Dan, gaze glued to Wade's face, jerked his head slightly to one side. "Staten Island?"

Wade nodded and then rolled his eyes. "Super-secret hyena den."

"Where exactly?"

"Don't know." At Dan's look of disbelief, he said more forcefully, "I *don't*. Crazy agents from the XIA already asked me. What's going on? Is this because we went to Edgemere? Doesn't make sense – that was Mad Eye territory, not the Bitches'."

Dan ignored him and turned away in frustration. If Wade was lying to protect his father, there was no way he was going to get the truth out of him. His knees threatened to buckle as a sudden wave of dizziness and nausea hit, reminding him he hadn't eaten anything since the chips in Cory's van.

Bass, who'd been standing nearby, said, "Danny, you look like shit. You seriously need to check in with your mom. Maybe see a doctor because damn."

Dan looked hopelessly at his best friend. "They're going to kill her."

Voice raised, Wade demanded, "Why?"

"Does it matter?"

Wade looked down, gaze shifting randomly, and Dan could practically hear the inner monologue as he tried to justify his father's actions. Wade lifted his head, indicating he'd gotten an idea. He pulled his holophone from his pocket and pressed a button. After a few rings, Cerberus' face appeared.

"What?"

"Hey, Dad," Wade said. "Where you at?"

The background of the holo – a windowless room somewhere – told Dan nothing about Cerberus' location, but the reverse wasn't true. Angry color suffused Cerberus' face when he realized Dan was present.

"This ain't none of your business, Wade," he growled. "Stay out of it, you hear me, boy?"

"Loud and clear," Wade replied, but his father had already ended the call.

The school bell rang as Wade was shoving the holophone back into his pocket. "You heard the man. I'm out."

Dan watched dazedly as Wade and his friends sauntered towards the school entrance. Within minutes, the campus was deserted except for Dan, Bass, and Freya's friends, all of whom, except Sandrew, were staring at Dan in expectation – of what, he didn't know.

"You're going to be late for class," he said woodenly to no one in particular.

Sandrew, who'd been fixated on his holophone, said, "I got this, guys."

If it was meant as a dismissal to the others, none of his friends chose to leave. Instead, they huddled together to get a better look at his holophone. It was in 2D mode, so Dan couldn't see whatever it was they were doing.

His stomach growled, loud and long. Bass riffled around in his backpack and then handed Dan a sandwich. "Sounds like you could use this."

Dan gave him a grateful look and barely unwrapped the sandwich before taking a huge, ravenous bite.

"I didn't want to say anything in front of Wade," Bass said, "but I think you should call the cops."

Mouth full, Dan's response, "Can't," was garbled. When he swallowed, he said loud enough for everyone to hear, "The XIA think they've been infiltrated, so we can't call them."

Bass's mouth dropped open. "The Xenofreak Intelligence Agency? What the hell have you gotten mixed up in?"

Cindy exhaled in annoyance. "To sum up: Freya's got a graft. Someone wants her dead because of it. Her cousin's in the XIA. Try to keep up."

As summations go, Cindy's was scarce on details, but Bass chose not to challenge her on it.

140

Dan finished hoovering the sandwich as Sandrew announced, "Alrighty then. I've got it narrowed down to two places in the killzone they could have taken her."

"How?" Bass asked with badly hidden skepticism.

"Magic," Sandrew replied. Jin nudged him with her elbow, so he relented. "We asked around in Hologame Club. Specifically, the New York branch of Holoventurers."

Bass bent his knees and held his arms out in a dramatic en garde pose. "You mean those steampunk douchebags who wander around fighting invisible monsters in the street?"

Sandrew's eyes went wide and he blinked deliberately a few times, effectively communicating his offense. Holoventurers was an augmented reality hologame where the players wore special goggles that enabled them to engage with characters and other players within a multitude of holoworlds laid out across actual world locations. Dan, who preferred to get his action from real life, had never understood the appeal. Unlike Bass, however, he didn't doubt that Sandrew had found something useful. The kid was weird, but crazy tech smart.

"Those *douchebags*," Jin snapped, "know every neighborhood in New York upwards and downwards. Even the most hardcore holoventurers avoid the xeno dens."

"Yeah," Cindy chimed in. "And FYI, you're standing in the middle of a herd of zombies, and they'd be eating your brains right now if you had any."

Bass wisely chose to ignore Cindy's comment.

"So now all we have to do," Kaye said, "is figure out how to mount a rescue mission."

"No." Dan shook his head adamantly. "You guys stay here. It's too dangerous."

Sandrew laughed. "Oh, we're not going. We're strictly support. Behind the scenes strategists if you will. We'll help you and Ass – I mean Bass – come up with a plan, and if you guys run into trouble, you can call us for advice. How's that?"

Dan's holophone was in his apartment and there was no way he was going home. His mother would tackle him to the ground if he tried to leave again. He turned to Bass.

"Your mom give you your phone back?"

"It's in jail for two more weeks."

Sandrew sighed as he unzipped a pocket on his backpack and produced a second holophone. "This is my backup in case my main one gets confiscated in class. Do not lose it."

Dan's smile stretched his swollen face and turned into a wince of pain. "Thanks."

"Put your hologame faces on," Jin said. "This is for Freya."

Chapter Thirty-three

The stairwell door opened on the top floor and Serb led Freya down a hallway past glass-enclosed offices – all of which were empty except one. In the low light from his holophone, she saw several people inside wearing holohelmets and waving their arms in the darkness like ninjas performing tai chi. They were either playing a hologame, which was unlikely, or processing data. Were they the cyberexploiters Maddy had mentioned?

Serb deposited her in a small room off the lobby and locked her in. There was no furniture, and she got a quick glimpse of stained linoleum and scuffed, dingy walls before the door shut her in darkness. The distinct odor of pine-scented ammonia suggested the place had once been a janitor's supply closet. She ran her hands blindly across the wall until she encountered a light switch and flipped it. To her surprise the light came on. Whoever was in charge must be keeping the building dark so the place seemed abandoned. Along with the light, there was an exhaust fan set in the ceiling. Its fan rattled and the halogen light buzzed annoyingly, but she much preferred the noise to the darkness.

She paced the short length and breadth of the room for hours, trying to focus her chaotic thoughts despite the dread and despair saturating her brain. If her survival depended on rescue from outside forces, the odds were not in her favor. Dan might still be alive, but the only entity with the power to truly help her was the XIA, and Ryan had told them in no uncertain terms that the agency was compromised. That meant Dan probably wouldn't even try to call them, and she didn't blame him.

With the acceptance that no one was coming came clarity. She couldn't fight her way out, nor could she escape, so her only chance was to out-think her kidnappers – and the clock was ticking. She methodically sorted through everything she knew about the enemy, eventually concentrating on the million-dollar question: why was she still alive? The most obvious reason was that they wanted something from her. Since they'd killed off all the other Falconot graftees, presumably without kidnapping and questioning them first, that thing was most likely information about Maddy Singh. Maddy had made it clear that she'd been a thorn in her father's side for some time now, and Freya's presence on the beach tied her to the Mad Eye queen.

The second possible reason had to do with what she'd read in the Matrixeno report. They knew Ryan was her cousin, and they knew he was XIA. They had to be considering what he would be willing to do to save her. If they were planning to ask him for ransom, payment would be information on the XIA.

Realizing she potentially had value to them set her mind somewhat at ease. She sat with her back against the wall and eventually dozed off. When the sound of a key turning woke her, she scrambled up off the floor and faced the door, trembling in terrified anticipation.

Daylight streaming in through the exterior windows silhouetted the woman Serb had referred to as Matron. She stood there with one hand on the doorknob, the other resting on the gun strapped to her hip. Her features – pointy nose, high cheekbones, and narrow chin – could only be described as "sharp." The whites of her empty eyes were tinted yellow, and her skin was sallow except for the purplish bruise on her jawline, which reminded Freya that Ryan had somehow escaped after Matron captured him at the beach.

"I need to go to the bathroom," Freya said.

"Tough." Matron opened the door wider. "Let's go."

Freya followed the tall woman down a long, wide hallway with glass walls, passing door after door of empty offices. Matron stopped at one of them and gestured for Freya to enter a large space that wasn't empty – there were three people seated at a conference table – Serb and the driver of the SUV at one end, and one bound and gagged at the other.

Mrs. Carson.

Chapter Thirty-four

Now that they knew where on Staten Island to look, the only remaining obstacle was transportation. Freya's friends went to class, while Dan and Bass walked across the street to discuss their options.

"Bus?" Bass suggested.

"Take all day."

"Taxi? Rydi?"

Dan made a face and rubbed his fingers together.

"Okay," Bass said. "Time and money are obviously factors. Hitchhike?"

Dan didn't respond; just stared towards the student parking lot. Bass must have realized what he was thinking, because he said, "That would be suicidal."

Dan couldn't suppress a sly grin. "But satisfying."

"Well," Bass drawled, "he did have to get gas on the way home the other night, so the tank's full. Burned through a lot of fuel losing that white van. Who *were* those guys anyway?"

"Long story. Tell you on the way."

They headed straight for Wade's jeep, which was splattered in mud from Edgemere. It wasn't locked – Wade figured rightly that none of the students at Temple Grandin would dare mess with it – not that anyone could possibly covet the ancient thing. It also didn't need a key to start it; a screwdriver had been jammed into the ignition switch for as long as Dan had known Wade. He'd been told that Wade had lost the keys, but he suspected the vehicle had been stolen in the first place.

And now it's gonna be stolen again, he thought as he turned the screwdriver.

Dan drove out of the parking lot while Bass watched out the window with a worried look on his face. "He's gonna know it was us."

"True." Dan clenched his jaw. "Kinda looking forward to the next time I see him."

Once the school was out of sight, Bass turned and settled in his seat. "So tell me what's going on."

During the drive to the first of the locations Sandrew had given them, Dan filled Bass in on everything that had happened. He expected his normally garrulous friend to bombard him with questions, but instead, Bass kept fidgeting and seemed distracted.

"Why are you doing that?" Dan asked, after the third or fourth time Bass twisted to look out the back window. They'd crossed the bridge onto Staten Island and had almost reached their destination.

"I think we're being followed," Bass said, "but it's hard to tell because the window is so dirty. Would it kill Wade to wash this POS once in a while?"

Dan looked into the rearview mirror, immediately noticing a white van two cars back.

"The van?"

"Yeah. Think it's them?"

"Don't know, but we're here."

He pulled onto the side of the road next to a chain link fence that surrounded the property, while Bass kept an eye on the white van.

"They turned," Bass reported. "Not them."

Dan nodded absently. He asked Bass to roll down his window so he could study the building and its large, nearly empty parking lot. There was a reflective film applied to the windows, making it impossible to see inside.

"Look at that," Bass said, pointing to a sign attached to the fence that read, "Danger, Keep Out." There were other warning signs proclaiming the property condemned.

"Doesn't look dangerous."

"Sandrew said this place is abandoned. Some kind of natural disaster."

"Someone's here. Cars in the parking lot look just like the ones they use." Not to mention Maddy had said her father's soldiers liked to squat in abandoned buildings.

"Maybe we should check out the second address Sandrew gave you," Bass said.

A slight breeze blew fresh air into the jeep through the open window. Dan took a deep breath and held it for a moment. "No. She's here."

146

Chapter Thirty-five

Other than the strip of duct tape over her mouth and severely mussed hair, Mrs. Carson didn't look any worse for wear. She struggled against her bonds and made desperate noises in her throat when Freya entered the room, but Serb waved his gun and said, "What did I just tell ya?"

Mrs. Carson subsided, but glared hatred in his direction.

Matron led Freya to the far side of the table. Freya glanced out the window at the back lot; the building was situated at the top of a steep slope overlooking a marshy field. The view must have been lovely when it was first built, but now it was marred by a huge hole in the slope that had claimed part of the parking lot, as if a giant had taken a scoop out of the ground like it was ice cream. The warning signs posted at the entrance to the property suddenly made sense. The building was poised at the edge of a precipice.

Matron pulled two chairs away from the table and shoved Freya into one of them before sitting next to her. She put a hand to her ear and said, "Ready."

Moments later, the door opened to admit three more men. Two were dressed like mercenaries, but the third wore the crisp, spotless clothing of a businessman. Freya had seen Philip Singh's image in the media enough to recognize him instantly. His lips were curved in a conciliatory smile, but she knew from Ryan and Maddy that he was a chameleon whose demeanor he could put on and take off at will.

"I'd like to apologize–" he began.

"Save it," Freya said, pleased that her voice only shook a little. "We both know it would be insincere."

The smile vanished. "Have it your way," he replied.

He looked at Serb, who stood, walked over to Mrs. Carson, and placed the gun against her temple. Mrs. Carson closed her eyes.

"Why are you doing this?" Freya asked.

147

"Just answer my questions truthfully and I'll let you both go."

It was a lie and she knew it, but there was no point calling him out on it.

"Fine," she said.

He took a deep breath and let it out. Freya thought she saw a flicker of regret in his eyes, but of course she couldn't trust that the emotion was real.

"Where is my son?" he asked.

Freya knew he meant Maddy but made a face like she had no idea what he was talking about.

His lips thinned. "You know him as the Mad Eye Queen."

"Last I saw her," Freya said, deliberately using Maddy's preferred gender pronoun, "she was on her yacht. That was yesterday morning before you attacked it."

"What were you doing there?"

"It's a long story."

"Sum it up," he snapped.

"She wanted to save me from you."

"Out of the goodness of *her* heart." It was not just a baldly sarcastic statement; he was asking why.

Freya shrugged. "She said you tried to kill her, too."

"That's neither here nor there. What did she tell the XIA?"

"That you were a monster."

His face transformed into a grotesque mask of unbridled fury. "I will choke the life out of you myself if you make one more foolish statement. What does the XIA know?"

Freya could barely hear her own response over the pounding of her heart. "That you killed all those people from my – from the Falconot Biomedical clinical trial."

"What evidence do they have?"

By now there was a very good chance his cyberexploiters, as Maddy had called them, had informed him of Maddy's Matrixeno hack. If Freya confirmed that the XIA knew about it, she would undoubtedly be dooming each of the high school boys who'd received the same graft as Dan.

"None," she said.

Singh smiled unpleasantly. "You're a terrible liar. It's the hesitation before answering that gives you away. Good prevarication requires fast thinking. Now tell the truth."

"They'll know it was you if you try to kill those Matrixeno boys."

"Like your little friend Daniel?" The smile grew even more unpleasant. "Matrixeno...that whole thing was my idea. Brilliantly devious, don't you think?"

"A little convoluted maybe."

The smile froze. "I don't think you fully understand how precarious your situation is."

"I think you're wrong."

A tic formed over his left eye. "How so?"

"I know you're going to kill me, which means I have nothing to lose. Your daughter's right. You *are* a monster."

Freya had never seen anyone gnash their teeth before. Singh's came together with a snap and an audible grinding as he flung his arms wide before abruptly aborting the movement and regaining control of himself.

He turned to Matron. "Verify that's all she knows."

He swept out of the room, his personal guards trotting to keep up.

Chapter Thirty-six

Dan wanted to rush into the building to find Freya, but Bass pointed out that he was unarmed, untrained, and unlikely to get lucky.

"We have to stick to the plan," he said. He pulled Sandrew's spare phone from his pocket and sent a quick text message. Moments later, a chiming sound announced the response.

Bass frowned. "He says to wait for backup."

"Backup?" Dan looked around. "Ask him–"

The phone chimed again. Bass read it aloud, "Left the you-know-whos a ton of breadcrumbs."

"Who does he mean – the XIA? And what does bread–"

The phone chimed a third time. Bass read, "Don't do anything stupid."

"That was probably from Cindy," Dan muttered.

He slumped in his seat, frustrated. The next several minutes seemed to crawl by, giving him time to study the exterior of the building. He took note of two security cameras as well as what appeared to be a solar panel on the roof. The "natural disaster" must have been pretty bad for the owners to abandon such pricey tech. He was about to ask Bass to find out how much longer they would have to wait when he heard something. "Is that a helicopter?"

Bass lifted his head. "I think so."

Things happened rapidly after that. Three unmarked law enforcement vehicles, lights flashing but without sirens, sped past. The helicopter landed in the parking lot. From Dan's vantage point, he could only see one of the vehicles as it pulled up to the building. Four armed personnel exited, leaving one to stand guard at the vehicle while the other three headed for the main entrance and forced their way in. Dan was staring at the scene, listening for gunfire when someone knocked on the driver's side window and he nearly jumped out of his skin.

Maddy Singh and her man Oscar stood there. She impatiently mimed for him to roll down the window, and he hastily complied.

"Is my father in there?" she asked.

"No idea," Dan replied. "Freya is, though."

"How do you know?"

"I smelled her."

Maddy's eyebrows twitched upward before she made a quick, ironic grimace indicating her willingness to believe his outrageous claim.

She tilted her head towards the guard. "That the XIA?"

Dan nodded. "Pretty sure."

She glanced at Oscar. "Are you familiar with this building?"

"Nope. Seen those cars before, though."

She squinted at the parking lot, and then looked towards the guard, whose back was turned and who had yet to notice them even though they were only about a hundred yards away. "One guard standing between my father's men and their getaway vehicles."

"Want I should drop him?" Oscar asked. "We could disable them."

Maddy seemed to be considering it, but then glanced at Dan and shook her head. "We're working *with* the XIA now."

Dan happened to be looking at the agent standing guard when the man finally spotted them. Dan saw the agent's lips move, and assumed he'd notified someone that they had an audience.

"Guard just made us," he said. Then something occurred to him. "Did you follow us here?"

Maddy acknowledged the question with an "mm" sound. "Easier than trying to track the XIA."

A moment later, she lifted her hands and stepped back from the jeep. Dan turned his head and saw a group of three helmeted agents approaching cautiously from the other side of the fence, guns raised and aimed at the jeep. When the leader caught sight of Maddy, he lowered his rifle, flipped up the visor on his helmet, and strode forward rapidly.

"What are you doing here?" It was Dragila.

"Followed the boy." Maddy nodded towards the jeep.

Dragila bent to look through the open window. "Why are *you* here, kid?"

"My friends are the ones that called you," Dan said.

Dragila looked mildly confused. "No one called us. We got a tip about a Hyena den that may be associated with the xenos that were killed in the conflict yesterday. Our analysts detected a flood of…are your friends hologamers?"

"Yeah."

151

One of the other agents stepped forward. "Where's Freya?"

Dan couldn't see his face behind the helmet, but he recognized Ryan's voice. "They knocked me out and took her."

"What?" Ryan exclaimed, ripping the helmet from his head.

Dan gave them an abbreviated version of Freya's kidnapping. Ryan grilled him for details until Dragila pointed out that he was repeating questions that had been asked and answered. Something about the interaction, maybe just because the authorities had been finally apprised of the situation, made Dan suddenly feel like crying. He looked down at his lap and fought it off.

"I think she's in there." He gestured towards the building.

Dragila rubbed his chin almost violently. "Nope. It's empty."

"Then why are those cars here?" Maddy asked.

"Ever heard of a park and ride?" Ryan said, and Dan couldn't tell if he was being sarcastic.

"We went floor by floor," Dragila said. "Place has been vacant for over a year. Sinkhole took the ground out from under the north side of the building and city records show no utility usage since then. Our helmets automatically scan for infrared and there were no heat signatures. Ground's too unstable for tunnels. She's not in there."

Maddy directed an inquiring look at Dan, who asserted, "She *was*."

"How do you know?" Ryan demanded.

Dan's certainty faded under Ryan's penetrating gaze. He looked away without answering. There was no way Freya's cousin would believe he'd picked up her scent like some kind of bloodhound.

"Alright," Dragila said with a disappointed sigh. He put a hand to his helmet. "Stand down. False alarm."

Maddy thrust a hand toward the SUVS. "At least run a few license plates before you call it a day."

"Already done," Dragila replied. "There's no evidence those vehicles belong to bad guys. C'mon Maddy, you know we're not in the business of chasing down weakass leads."

"Well, that is all my father is going to leave in his wake, so I suggest you begin doing so."

"You know what?" Ryan said, glaring at Maddy. "I'm starting to question whether this is all a game to you. We have zero confirmation that your father is even involved."

"Yes, agent Boardman, because I attacked *myself* yesterday for shits and giggles."

Ryan started to respond, but Dragila held up a hand. "We need to sit down and—" he stopped, frowned, and stared past Maddy's shoulder as his head tilted to one side. "You see that?"

Dan looked out the open driver's side window just in time to spot a weird shimmer in the air, like heat rising from the tarmac on a hot day, only this mirage appeared to be moving right past them. He heard faint popping sounds like tires make when they encounter pebbles in the road.

Dragila put a hand to his helmet. "Lo, lift off! We've got an invisible bogey heading south of our location!"

Dragila and his agents sprinted for their vehicles. He looked over his shoulder and pointed at Dan as he ran. "Go home! Stay there!"

Dan reluctantly nodded, but the agent had already turned away. The rotors on the helicopter began to turn.

"Your father has one of those UAAVs?" he asked Maddy, who was standing as if frozen, a calculating look on her face. She ignored him; lips compressed as she watched the agents get into their vehicles.

"What are your orders?" Oscar prompted.

Other than a minuscule shake of the head, she didn't respond. The four of them waited silently as the XIA sped past. Maddy's gaze stayed with the helicopter until the noise faded away and then found the building again.

"It's a decoy," she murmured. "To lure them away."

Oscar nodded slowly. "I agree."

"Daddy's in there. They wouldn't go to so much trouble if he wasn't."

Dan pointed to the roof of the building. "Looks like a solar panel, which means those," he moved his arm to point at one of the security cameras, "might be working."

"You're right, he knows we're here. We should retreat – or at least appear to." She turned to Dan. "I strongly urge you to *actually* leave."

"Why? What are you going to do?"

"That's none of your concern."

"You gonna shoot shit up? Because *Freya* is my concern."

She and Oscar exchanged a glance. "I'm sorry, Dan," Maddy said, looking genuinely distraught, "but she's already dead."

With one last sympathetic look, she turned and walked away, Oscar at her heels.

When they'd disappeared around the corner, Bass asked, "We going home?"

Dan took a deep breath. The breeze coming in through the open window held no hint of Freya's scent, but the memory of it was strong. He turned the screwdriver to start the engine.

153

"Hell no."

Chapter Thirty-seven

After Singh left the room, Matron made a big show of cracking her knuckles while staring at Freya with a small, cruel smile that was nowhere near as terrifying as Singh's. Before she could really get into the role of inquisitor, however, a helicopter buzzed overhead, and all hell broke loose.

Matron put a hand to her ear and barked, "Status!" and then after listening for a moment told Serb and the driver, "One helo, three ground incoming. ETA less than a minute." She pointed to the driver, "Take Alpha to the cloak room. I'll deploy the decoy. Everyone else in the file room – leave no indication we were here! Go, go, go!"

Serb yanked Mrs. Carson up from her seat while the driver ran around the conference table and out the door behind Matron. Freya, propelled by a rush of adrenaline – if the helicopter got this kind of reaction, it could only be good for her – jumped to her feet. Serb pulled Mrs. Carson towards the door, giving Freya a look that told her she'd better cooperate. She hurried behind them down the hallway to one of the few rooms with solid walls. Unlike the glass-enclosed rooms Freya had seen, this room wasn't empty; there were several rows of file cabinets. Serb dragged Mrs. Carson to the furthest row as more people hastily entered the room.

The file cabinets appeared ordinary; four wide-drawered units per row, but when Serb slammed the palm of his hand against the nearest one, the side opened like a door. What appeared on the outside to be individual cabinets was actually one long hollow structure embedded a couple of feet into the floor.

Matron popped her head into the room and barked, "Serb!"

He barely had time to turn towards her when she lobbed a small black box at him and disappeared again. He caught the box with one hand, and then slapped his other onto the back of Freya's head, forcing it down as he pushed her inside the narrow file cabinet. A block of wood functioned as a step. There was barely enough room for her to stand upright without hitting her head on the ceiling. Mrs. Carson came next; Freya took her arm to assist her to the far end of the space. After the three of them crowded inside, Serb shut and bolted the door, and they waited in pitch blackness, the only sound the labored breathing of Mrs. Carson.

Freya lifted her hands and felt her way to the old woman's face, where she gently began working at peeling the duct tape away from her mouth. She didn't want Serb to figure out what she was doing, so by necessity, it was slow, tedious work. Once the last of the tape came free, she was afraid Mrs. Carson would say something, or begin breathing through her mouth – a change that would surely be heard – but the old woman was too shrewd to give herself away.

Freya then began to work on the tape binding Mrs. Carson's wrists. It was getting warm and stuffy inside the cabinets. With no source of fresh air, their time inside would have to be limited. She could only estimate how much had passed; maybe fifteen minutes since the helicopter had arrived.

A small green light suddenly appeared in the ceiling. It must have been the "all clear," signal because Serb unbolted and opened the door but then stopped short, blocking the entrance. Freya looked past Mrs. Carson directly at the gun Matron held.

"The printer," Matron said, holding out her free hand.

"What's going on?" Serb responded warily.

"Guess who's sitting outside in your son's jeep?" Matron asked in a deceptively conversational tone.

"My – my son?" Serb sounded dumbfounded. "I told him not to–"

"Not your good-for-nothing spawn, you moron. It's the boy from last night. The one I ordered you to kill."

Serb lowered his head and hunched his shoulders submissively. He held out the black box Matron had tossed to him earlier, but before she could take it, he suddenly fell backwards into Mrs. Carson, pulling the door shut and flipping the bolt. Matron got off one shot before it slammed.

Darkness enclosed them once again, only this time it was Serb whose breathing filled the space as he gasped and groaned in pain.

Mrs. Carson didn't miss a beat. "Finish this, would you?" she said, nudging Freya with her still-bound hands.

Freya began picking at the tape again, but then realized there was no point being subtle about it and bent to tear at it with her teeth.

She kept expecting gunfire to strafe the file cabinet, but the fact that she'd heard nothing from the outside – and from what little she knew about Matron, she expected to hear some angry shouting at the very least – told her the cabinets were soundproof. Probably they were bulletproof, too. They'd clearly been manufactured to appear innocuous; something found in

156

every building across the country, but secretly intended as temporary safe rooms, although she thought "room" was hardly accurate. One thing was certain, if the door could be opened from the outside, Matron would have.

Even as her thoughts traveled all over the map assessing the minutia, she clung to the only good thing she'd learned: *Dan was alive.* The jeep Matron had referred to could only belong to Wade, which meant Serb was in actuality Cerberus, Wade's father. She should have made the connection, but even if she'd had, the knowledge wouldn't have made a difference. Serb was a Hyena under the influence of his xenograft, or at least he had been; his disobedience demonstrated that Matron didn't completely control him.

When the duct tape tore loose and Mrs. Carson's hands were free, the old woman said, "I'm a nurse. Do you have a holophone? I need light."

"You gonna help me?" Serb's voice was thick, like his throat was full of mucus; his words almost unintelligible except for the tone of disbelief.

"I help you – you help us. Deal?"

Serb coughed wetly. A light flared from the holophone in his hand. Mrs. Carson took the phone and turned its light on him. Over her shoulder, Freya could see he'd slumped sideways in the small space, his back against one wall, knees jammed into his chest. From the amount of blood alone – his camouflage print shirt had soaked it up like a sponge – she suspected it was a mortal wound. That much blood in such a short amount of time did not bode well for his survival, especially given that they were trapped, and the enemy only had to wait until they ran out of air.

Freya couldn't see Mrs. Carson's face, but his condition must have been all over it, because he said, "I'm done, but you can get out, get a message to my–" he stopped, choking as blood gushed from his mouth.

"Don't try to talk," Mrs. Carson said, "I need you to–"

"No! *Listen.* Once Alpha's evacuated, they'll activate the failsafes and you'll have ten minutes." He looked up at Freya, eyes beginning to glaze over. "I'm sorry. My son…tell him…"

"That you love him. Yes. I promise."

"You need to go…" His voice trailed away to barely a whisper, and his eyes closed. A gentle sigh left his lips as he died.

Mrs. Carson put two fingers on his neck to check his pulse, and then felt around until she located his holster. She removed his gun and said, "Help me up."

Freya grasped her elbow and heaved upward. Once the old woman had gained her feet, she looked at Serb's holophone and muttered, "Passcode protected."

"They might be waiting for us." Mrs. Carson lifted the gun. "You ready?"

Suddenly the cramped space seemed awfully inviting, but Freya responded, "Don't have much choice, whatever the failsafes are."

Mrs. Carson stepped over Serb's body onto the wood block, unbolted the door, and opened it a crack. Nothing happened, so she was emboldened to open it further and lean out. After a moment, she stepped over the threshold and waved for Freya to follow.

After Freya gingerly stepped over Serb, she noticed the black box next to his body. It was clearly important, so she took it with her as she joined Mrs. Carson in the abandoned file room. They were directly opposite the stairwell, so they darted across the hallway without encountering anyone. Freya was afraid Mrs. Carson would need help navigating each step, but the old woman tucked the gun and holophone in her pockets and gripped the rail with both hands, descending like a hellhound was nipping at her heels.

When they reached the ground floor, Freya peered through the small rectangular window in the stairwell door. Seeing no movement, she cautiously opened the door and poked her head out. There was no one in the lobby, so she held the door for Mrs. Carson, whispering, "All clear."

But it wasn't.

Chapter Thirty-eight

Dan drove a short distance and turned left, passing the parked white van. Neither Maddy nor Oscar appeared to be inside; they would be hidden nearby watching to see which vehicle her father got into so they could target it.

He turned right and drove another block before parking again. "They can't see us from here."

"We can't see them, either," Bass pointed out.

"I know." Dan reached for the door handle.

"Where you going?"

"Just getting a closer look."

Bass's moan of frustration followed him as he jumped out and crossed the street. The buildings in this area seemed largely industrial; rows of storage units, prefabricated buildings, and steel Quonset huts crowded together on small gravel lots. The dearth of cars suggested the businesses were victims of the recession or the employees were victims of automation. Either way, Dan was glad no one was around to see him skulking between and around the structures.

He traversed the entire block until he reached the last building, a windowless prefab with rusted corrugated metal walls. Peeking around the corner gave him perfect line of sight to the front of the abandoned office complex.

"Surprise, surprise," he muttered as he spotted a dozen or so men and women hurrying towards the parked vehicles, all carrying duffel bags and wearing various tech that suggested they were the cyberexploiters Maddy had referred to on her yacht. Freya was not among them, nor was Philip Singh. Behind them marched the mercs; ten men with guns who were either guarding or herding the technicians – or both. After the men and women piled into all but one of the SUVs, four of the mercs got into their respective driver's seats and started the engines.

Dan flattened himself against the wall as the SUVs drove past, and then looked again. The six remaining mercs had moved into a protective formation between the last SUV and the main door of the building. He eyed the guns each of them held; assault rifles of some kind. He was just thinking there was literally nothing he could do but stay impotently hidden when he felt a hand on his shoulder.

He knew it was Maddy before he turned. She made a "shh" sound against the index finger pressed to her lips. Oscar waved a hand and three armed men materialized from the shadows behind him.

"You didn't think I was out here all by my lonesome, did you?" Maddy asked quietly.

Dan hadn't thought about it, but there was plenty of room in Maddy's van for the squad of xenofreaks awaiting her orders. He relinquished his spot to her, and she took over surveilling the building.

They didn't wait long.

"*There* you are," she drawled.

Dan knew without being told who she meant. "Is Freya with him?"

"No." There was no sympathy in the short utterance. A downward twitch of the corners of her mouth betrayed nothing but resolve.

She nodded to Oscar, who immediately rounded the side of the building and ran in a crouch towards the remaining SUV, keeping it between him and the mercs. His men fanned out behind him and to Dan, their shoes striking the tarmac sounded overly loud, but they made it to within fifty yards of the goal before one of the mercs caught sight of them. The man swung around but immediately dropped to the ground, a gentle "fwup" sound the only indication he'd been shot. Despite the precaution of using silencers, the remaining mercs didn't fail to notice their fallen comrade. They spotted Oscar's assault force and opened fire.

Looking past Maddy's shoulder, Dan caught a quick glimpse of Philip Singh and the woman accompanying him before they dashed back into the building. The door had been open only briefly, but a moment later his supercharged olfactory system picked up the scent of Freya's xenograft.

He couldn't tell whether she was alive or dead, but he *knew* she was in that building.

A stray bullet buried itself into the wall a few feet away from them with a granular spray of stucco, but Maddy didn't even flinch. Her face had taken on a look of fierce desperation as one by one, her men fell. Oscar, the last of them, dove to the ground behind the SUV and began firing under it, targeting the legs of the mercs.

To Dan's right, the jeep suddenly appeared and screeched to a halt.

"Get in!" Bass yelled.

Before Dan could react, Maddy yanked the driver's door open, grasped the front of Bass's shirt, and hauled him out. As she jumped in, Dan lunged for the handle of the rear door. He hurled himself across the back seats just before she stomped the electrigas pedal to the floor. The old jeep still had some life in her; Dan had only seconds to come to terms with his decision as they accelerated towards the building. The two mercs that were still standing shifted their attention from Oscar's position behind the SUV to the new threat barreling towards them.

Maddy bent sideways as bullet holes peppered the windshield and it became opaque with cracks. Dan scooted onto the floor just before they collided with something and he caught a quick, distorted glimpse of an upside-down face out the side window. The jeep shuddered onward.

If there'd been time for Dan to form an assumption about Maddy's intentions, he would have settled on "rescue." As it turned out, she had more of a kamikaze intervention in mind.

Chapter Thirty-nine

At the first sound of gunfire, Freya and Mrs. Carson retreated back into the stairwell. Freya pressed her cheek to the door, keeping watch out the little window. She couldn't see who was shooting, but bullets pierced the glass wall at the front entrance until it shattered, sending fragments raining down into the lobby. Philip Singh, bent at the waist with arms folded behind his head for protection, stumbled inside. Matron and one of the mercenaries provided cover fire for him until Matron took a bullet and went down. Singh slipped on the glass and fell before scrambling on his hands and knees to shelter behind the huge curved reception desk. The last remaining mercenary joined him behind the desk as the firefight raged on outside.

There was a pause in the gunfire and Matron stirred. She lifted her head to look outside and then suddenly rolled out of Freya's field of view as Wade's jeep tore through the metal doorjamb and crashed into the reception desk. Steam belched from the engine's damaged radiator. Freya held her breath waiting for the driver, presumably Dan, to exit the jeep, but had to exhale before he appeared.

"Don't be hurt," she whispered to herself, free hand hovering over the door handle. She watched helplessly as the mercenary made his way out from behind the desk and approached the jeep.

She turned to Mrs. Carson, about to plead for Serb's gun, but the old woman had been exploring the stairwell and was standing at the end of a narrow passageway near a second door with the words, "Emergency Exit" painted on it in large red text.

"Over here!" she stage-whispered. "There's another door!"

A shot rang out and Freya whirled to look back out the window. Oscar was standing over the mercenary's prone form. Even though he must have shot the man point blank from behind, he kicked the gun out of the dead man's slack hand. It scattered broken glass as it slid across the floor, coming to rest up against the reception desk. Oscar then stalked to the jeep, opened the door, and reached inside to help the driver. Maddy Singh wriggled out past the deployed airbags, swiped a hand under her bloodied nose, and smoothed her mussed hair.

How she'd ended up behind the wheel of Wade's jeep was irrelevant; Freya now wanted nothing more than to escape. Her intention to join Mrs. Carson was thwarted, however, when out of the corner of her eye she saw a bloody hand reach out from behind the reception desk for the mercenary's gun. Philip Singh was about to get the drop on his daughter, something Freya couldn't in good conscience allow to happen. She jerked the door open and shouted, "He's there!"

She couldn't point because she had the door handle in one hand and was still holding the black box in the other, but she gestured with the box towards the desk.

Singh's shaking hand hovered over the gun.

"Give me a reason," Oscar said.

With a grunt, Singh lifted his arms and got slowly to his feet in apparent surrender, but he held something small in his left hand.

"This is a dead man's switch," he enunciated loudly, thrusting the hand forward. "You shoot, we all go boom."

The failsafes, Freya thought. Serb had warned them, and now she recalled the conversation aboard Maddy's yacht regarding Singh's security protocol; how the last building that had been breached by the XIA had been deliberately destroyed by arson. This building was situated so close to that sink hole in the parking lot, a strategically placed explosive charge would topple the entire structure, effectively burying any fingerprint or DNA evidence.

Freya hesitated in the doorway, but Maddy caught her eye and then distinctly dropped her gaze to the black box. With the hand that she held behind her back, she surreptitiously gestured that Freya go back into the stairwell.

Freya did so, and quickly made her way to where Mrs. Carson lingered by the emergency exit. Additional writing on the door proclaimed that an alarm would sound if they opened it, but nothing happened when they stepped out into the sunshine.

A black SUV was parked in front of the destroyed main entrance, surrounded by fallen xenofreak mercenaries. It was a horrific scene, and Freya only perused it long enough to establish that none of the bodies were moving and in need of help – or that they posed any danger.

She and Mrs. Carson circumnavigated the site and crossed the parking lot to the road. There were no cars, parked or otherwise. The industrial buildings lining the streets had no discernible activity whatsoever, that is until a lone figure stepped out from behind a rusty old building and lifted his arms in greeting.

"Hey!" he cried. "You guys okay?"

It was Bass, Dan's friend.

Freya abandoned Mrs. Carson to jog over to him.

"Where's Dan?" Freya and Bass spoke at the same time.

"Aw, man," Bass said. "He was in Wade's jeep."

"I didn't see him," she replied, taking a couple of steps backward and beginning to turn. From behind, Mrs. Carson placed a cautionary hand on her arm. Freya fought off the urge to ignore her wordless warning. There was nothing she could do if she went back.

Bass swore colorfully, but then said, "He's probably okay. Head's hard as a rock. You see Maddy?"

"Yeah, she's fine. Well, I mean, she's in a stand-off with her psychopath dad at the moment, but otherwise…" she shrugged and let out an exhausted sigh. "Can I use your phone? I need to call the XIA."

"Oh, they were here." He pulled a phone from his pants pocket but held onto it. "Went inside and didn't find anything."

"So they just left?"

"Kind of." He rolled his eyes. "They followed an invisible something-or-other, but Maddy said it was a decoy so her dad could get away."

"It was. They need to come back." She held her hand out for the phone.

"Mandy."

Ryan's voice came from above them. Freya heard that soft whirring noise the invisible drone had made and looked up and around, but it didn't make itself visible this time.

"Where are you?" she asked.

"A few minutes out. Sent the drone ahead. You alright?"

"I'm fine, but you should know Philip Singh is threatening to blow up the building. Dan, Maddy and Oscar are in there with him."

"Roger that. We'll pick you up, but in the meantime, whatever you do, don't lose that black box, you hear me?"

The urgency in his voice told Freya her decision to hang onto it had been a good one. She nodded and tightened her grip on the handle. "Hurry."

Ryan didn't respond, but the whirring faded away. From the sound of it, the drone was headed for the office building.

Chapter Forty

The impact that stopped the jeep's forward momentum slammed Dan like a ragdoll into the back of the front seats. His ribs struck the central console, knocking the wind out of him. Face mashed into the filthy carpet, dazed and bruised, he struggled to breathe for several minutes. He heard the gunshot and was aware that Maddy was unharmed and had gotten out of the vehicle, but it was Freya's voice – and her mouth-watering scent – that jolted him out of his stupor.

He got to his knees and painfully straightened his torso, looking out the window in time to see Philip Singh raise his arm and declare – what? Something about a dead man's switch?

There were two bodies on the lobby floor; a man face-down about ten feet away, and a woman lying on her side facing the far wall. Freya was standing in the doorway to the stairwell. Then he saw Maddy wave her back inside. As Freya withdrew, he was overcome with a profound sense of relief.

She's safe.

Maddy and her father's angrily raised voices echoed throughout the lobby. Dan definitely didn't want to call attention to himself, so he levered his backside onto the seat and turned to the door facing away from them. The sides of the jeep hadn't impacted with anything; nevertheless, the door wouldn't open. He squeezed his torso painfully between the front seats to try the driver's door, but it too refused to budge. The driver's door window had been shattered but climbing out that way would not be inconspicuous. To get out, he would have to exit on the right side of the jeep in full view of Philip Singh.

He subsided onto the back seat and sat there for a few minutes weighing the pros and cons of revealing himself. He finally decided that if he got out now, Singh might demand he stay, but as long as Oscar held him at gunpoint, Singh had no credible way of stopping Dan from leaving.

He reached for the door handle but then heard something out the shattered driver's side window that made him hesitate. He'd anticipated that Freya would alert the authorities, and had been halfway expecting to hear sirens, but instead picked up a faint sound he'd heard before; that of a drone.

He peered out into the gloom of the lobby but saw nothing. It had to be the XIA. They were watching and listening, which meant they were either here or coming back. He sighed and decided to stay put until they arrived. Best not to provoke Singh if he could help it.

The argument in the lobby had continued apace, but he'd mostly ignored it as irrelevant, highly personal family drama.

Then Singh said, "There's still time to make a deal."

"With you?" Maddy laughed. "Let me guess: I let you go, I'm back in the will?"

"More than that. I'll throw in an allowance. Hell, you want a position in the company? It's yours."

Oscar, who hadn't spoken a word during the argument, said, "She don't believe you."

"No one asked for your opinion," Singh replied coldly.

"No one had to." Maddy sniffed. "Oscar's opinion is always welcome. Not to mention his advice. You should really be nicer to staff. Fosters loyalty."

"So does fear." Singh's eyes shifted to Oscar, his former employee. "How's your mother? Still visit her every week at Desert Hills? So many of those places hire substandard help. Puts the residents in such a vulnerable position."

"She passed," Oscar said. "The day before I met Maddy, just so you know. But thanks for asking."

Maddy shook her head, staring at her father. "You just can't help yourself, can you? You are a horrible human being."

"Oh, don't act so sanctimonious. You've done things, don't think I don't know."

"I have," Maddy admitted, "but not for my own selfish purposes. I had a community of outcasts to protect – from people like you."

"Xenofreaks aren't outcasts," Singh replied. "They're abominations."

"See, that's what I don't understand. You hate us, yet you're perfectly happy experimenting with xenoaugmentation. You *had* a graft."

"I still do." His raised his right hand, the one holding the dead man's switch, and pulled the sleeve down to reveal a xenograft on his forearm.

166

Dan couldn't see it very well, but it looked like golden fur. Everyone knew Singh had previously gotten a crocodile graft which had to be removed because of the supertyphoid.

"Why would you get another one?" Maddy exclaimed. "It makes no sense."

"Doesn't it? I presume you were the one responsible for the hack into one of my subsidiary businesses yesterday?"

Maddy shrugged. "Matrixeno? Yes, that was me."

"So you're aware of its objective?"

"To find Freya."

"That, yes, but there's much more to it. A xenograft, depending on the type and the bioengineering method, doesn't just confer its immune properties to the graftee, it can actually influence human behavior. The Matrixeno boys would not be able to control themselves in the presence of a naked mole rat graftee. A woman with a hyena graft has almost total control over a man with one. My new graft is lion skin. Did you know the lion is the hyena's biggest enemy? Hyenas aren't afraid of much, but they respect the mighty lion. How do you think I got the Bitches to obey me?" He glanced over at the body of the woman. "It's actually quite exciting, and Matrixeno is on the cutting edge of the research. That is, now that Falconot Biomedical is out of the picture."

Dan bit his lip, unsure if Singh's reference to the company that provided Freya's graft could be considered an admission of wrongdoing. The XIA's drone was still out there, likely recording every word. If Singh had given them enough to arrest him, though, surely they would have burst in and done so.

"I knew it," Maddy said, voice subdued. "You're already richer than God, so the only thing left is power. You won't be happy until every person on the planet is under your boot heel. King of the lions."

Singh snorted. "I like that. Has a nice ring to it."

"But why blow up Poppy's Pier? How does killing thousands of xenos give you power?"

"I was *not* responsible for that. Honestly, why doesn't anyone believe me?"

"Did it burn just now? When the word "honestly" crossed your lips?"

"Listen," Singh said. "I literally found out about it after you showed up at the pier in your yacht. *You*, and the XIA agents you teamed up with, were the only reason I was even looped in."

"Assuming that's true, it doesn't negate the fact that you sent your soldiers after me."

167

"I was just making sure you didn't interfere." He pointed at Oscar. "You were there. Did I give them the kill order?"

Oscar shrugged. "You didn't have to. It's what they do."

Singh let out a frustrated growl. "I did not blow up the pier."

"Then who did?"

The look in Singh's eyes reminded Dan of a cornered animal. "They'll kill me if I tell you."

Maddy began to laugh. It started out as a chuckle but escalated into a full-throated guffaw. Singh's face suffused with angry color. When her laughter subsided enough for her to speak, she spat, "Liar, liar pants on fire."

Singh looked away but said nothing.

"These are the facts." Maddy held up her index finger. "Fournier set the super typhoid loose on the city." Her middle finger joined the first. "The resulting riots prompted Governor Koontz to declare martial law, and he ordered the National Guard to round up every xeno in the five boroughs and take them to Poppy's Pier." Her ring finger went up. "In the meantime, Congressman Abbott, whose testimony at the subcommittee for xeno regulation would have scorched the earth you and your cronies squat on, was kidnapped and also taken to the pier." She raised her pinky finger. "*Someone* took advantage of the perfect opportunity to kill two birds with one stone by blowing it to smithereens."

"Stop," Singh said. "*Maybe* this person's objective was simply to expose Abbott to the typhoid. *Maybe* the rest of it wasn't in this person's wheelhouse."

"You want to convince me? Then answer the question. Who *was* at the wheel?" Maddy spread her hands wide and held them there.

Singh never got a chance to respond to his daughter's query. A shot rang out, and his head snapped back violently, a dark smudge at his temple. The dead man's switch clattered to the floor before Singh's body collapsed. Dan saw the gun in Matron's hand just as a muffled boom shook the building. Maddy and Oscar sprinted past as he grasped the door handle and pulled. The door wouldn't open, so he hurled himself into the front seat, knowing as he did so that he was out of time.

Chapter Forty-one

During the wait for Ryan to return, Freya threw modesty to the wind and found a secluded corner in the gravel lot to finally pee. Afterward she asked if Mrs. Carson needed to go, but the old woman smirked and replied, "I left them a puddle in the room they had me in."

The XIA caravan of vehicles arrived on the scene full tilt, the lead car decelerating in a hard skid. They parked along the main road leading to the office building rather than in the parking lot. A dozen armed agents jumped out and congregated in the street. As Freya, Mrs. Carson, and Bass hurried over, a large, unassuming van pulled up and someone inside threw the back doors open. The agents quickly gathered around it; Freya guessed it was a mobile surveillance unit, the kind undercovers would sit in for hours or days at a time. As she got closer, Ryan broke from the ranks and met her with a rough hug. "Sure you're okay?"

"Yeah. I mean, I know this isn't a priority, but do you have any water? They didn't give us anything to eat or drink. Oh, and this is Mrs. Carson, and Bass, Dan's friend." Freya decided now was not the time to go into how and why they had become involved.

Ryan nodded by way of greeting and told Freya, "I'm sure we got something. May I?" He held his hand out for the black box and she relinquished it to him.

He wove his way through the crowd of agents and disappeared inside the van. Instead of returning, however, he leaned out, called, "Amanda!" and waved her over.

The crowd of agents parted to let her through, and when she reached the van, she was surprised that Ryan gestured for her to get in. There were three other agents crowded inside, Dragila, Cougar, and a slim, short-haired woman sitting at a control console, but she hardly noticed her surroundings as her gaze was drawn immediately to a holo playing out in the center of the space.

"These are the facts," Maddy said to her father.

Freya turned to Ryan. "Where's Dan?"

"We think he's in the jeep." He handed her a bottle of water. "You need to tell us everything."

Freya tilted her head back to take a long drink, half listening to Maddy, half trying to think how to explain the last few days. She lowered the bottle and looked at the holo just in time to see Matron roll over and shoot Philip Singh in the head.

Everyone in the van gasped as the dead man's switch left Singh's hand. A dull concussive sound, like a distant clap of thunder, rumbled ominously. When it faded away, it seemed for a moment that nothing was going to happen. Freya covered her nose and mouth with her hands, breath held as she stared out the front windshield. Then Maddy and Oscar burst from the building at a dead run. Behind them, the wall of windows shattered, sparkling like glitter as the entire four-story structure listed to one side.

There was no sign of Dan. Freya's shoulders slumped in abject hopelessness.

"Get the drone out of there!" Dragila shouted.

The slim woman grasped a joystick and muttered, "Gonna be close."

Freya shifted her gaze back to the holo, still live recording the event. Debris was falling everywhere in the lobby, deep cracks sprouting up and down the walls. As the drone retreated, the scene shifted in a disorienting blur. The ground caved in, flipping the jeep on its side. She caught the barest glimpse of a shadowy, shocked face through the window before the drone emerged into the sunshine.

A cacophony of grating, groaning, and snapping sounds reverberated through the air as the building toppled and slid down the slope in a cloud of dust. Half of the parking lot crumbled and shifted backward, taking with it the remaining SUV and the bodies of the mercenaries. In less than a minute, the entire complex had been reduced to a jumbled ruin of mangled steel and crushed concrete.

Chapter Forty-two

Sirens. Fire trucks. News helicopters and drones. Rescue personnel with cadaver dogs. Freya sat on a patch of dried grass at the side of the road, numb to her surroundings.

Maddy and Oscar took advantage of the pandemonium to disappear. Mrs. Carson had complained of chest pain and was taken by ambulance to the hospital. Bass was picked up by his mother, and Freya's had been notified that she was okay. Dan's parents were on their way and she was dreading it.

There was a commotion near an area the dogs had been investigating, and one of the paramedics rushed over with an armful of large black plastic bags. Freya got to her feet and walked away from it all, at first with no destination in mind, but then she made her way to the rusty metal building where she'd met up with Bass. At the back of the lot a chain link fence had been built along another slope – or rather, the far side of the same slope that had just collapsed. She followed the fence until she found what she was looking for; a hole big enough for her to duck through. She plowed downhill through high, wild grass and bushes until she encountered a narrow dirt trail.

She'd seen the trail out the conference room window and knew that it wound around the marshy field at the bottom of the slope. She trudged along the path to its highest point. From there, she got a fresh perspective on the devastation. What was left of the building had plowed a deep furrow in the marshland, settling, and possibly still sinking, into the mud. The top two floors had been reduced to a pile of rubble, but the bottom half appeared to be somewhat intact. The parking lot tarmac had cracked into dozens of chunks, some jutting vertically out of the newly formed slope, and some just resting on it like puzzle pieces. The rescuers, attached to safety ropes, were concentrated there. From the footprints in the mud, the human and canine rescuers hadn't ventured beyond that section of the crisis zone. There were three or four robo-spiders crawling through the wreckage, testing its stability, as well as several mini drones imaging the rubble to produce a holo.

Freya focused on the partially intact portion of the building. Her mind's eye flashed back to the glimpse she'd gotten of the jeep and Dan's face, but she shook the memory off. She knew the odds of his having survived were slim to none, and she most definitely did not want to be the one to discover his body, but something about the wreckage drew her. Without making a conscious decision to do so, she continued down the trail.

As she got closer to the debris, she heard voices calling out for her to stop. She forged onward, no longer under the influence of the shock-induced stupor that had compelled her forward thus far. Now it was fear that spurred her. The exact same fear she felt in Dan's presence.

Her steps slowed as the dirt became mud that sucked at her boots. She picked her way along little islands of broken cement, advancing toward a black hole in the rubble. One of the robo-spiders appeared at the top of a steel beam that lay across two chunks of concrete, the way a crossbeam rested on pillars to form a doorway. The spider didn't say anything, probably because it wasn't equipped with a speaker, but she knew its handler had sent it to block her way. She ignored it, fixated on the hole – and the terror it invoked.

"Amanda!"

She looked over her shoulder. Ryan was running down the trail. His headlong impetus sent him ploughing into the mud. He lost a shoe and fell about twenty yards away, looking up at her from all fours.

"Get back," he said, breathing hard from exertion.

Freya shook her head. "He's in there."

"Mandy…"

"He's *not* dead." She blinked repeatedly to keep from tearing up. "He's not. I can feel it."

"Can we get a drone here?" That was obviously not directed at her, but then he said, "Just wait, okay? We'll check it out safely."

The drone arrived moments later. It shone a bright light into the hole and flew slowly inside. Ryan got to his feet and made his way to where Freya waited. He put a muddy arm around her, and she leaned against him. After a couple of minutes, she heard a faint buzzing sound coming from his head; someone was speaking to him through his earbug.

He let out a short, astonished breath, said, "Okay," and then squeezed her.

"You were right. He's in there. Not conscious, but the drone registered a heartbeat and respiration. Excavation team's on its way."

172

Chapter Forty-three

Dan woke up in a hospital bed, the sole occupant of a dimly lit, sterile grey and blue room. He remembered regaining consciousness several times prior. Once when they pulled him from the mud and strapped him to a stretcher, once in a helicopter, and once just after he'd arrived at the ER.

He had a headache, and his right leg, suspended from a rope and pulley device, hurt like hell. He vaguely remembered the doctor explaining that he had a mild concussion and two uncomplicated fractures in his lower leg. The bed rail had symbols on it, and he found and pushed the call button. A nurse came in and asked if he was in pain. At his affirmative response, she administered some medication. He dozed off.

When he woke again, his parents were sitting in uncomfortable looking armchairs near the windows. He and his mother spoke for a while. She seemed reluctant to talk about what he'd been through, and he was okay with that; his father was uncommunicative, as always. They left when darkness fell.

In the morning, a "hostess" brought him breakfast. He was famished and inhaled the tasteless meal, even the Jell-O, which he hadn't eaten since he was in elementary school. Afterward, a different nurse came in to check on him.

"A couple of XIA agents are here to see you, apparently. Are you up for that?"

He was actually anxious for it. "Yes."

The agents were Dragila and a woman he introduced as Agent Fox. She got right to it.

"Good morning Mr. Corvi. I hope your injuries are on the mend." She set a holorecorder down on his wheeled bed side table and turned it on.

"Interview with Daniel Corvi, age eighteen," she said. "Present are Supervising Agent Shasta Fox and Agent Jason Alton. Mr. Corvi, do I have your consent to digitally document this interview?"

He raised his eyebrows but said, "Yes."

She continued. "On behalf of the Xenofreak Intelligence Agency, I would like to commend you for your contribution to the resolution of a long, difficult investigation into the activities of Philip Singh. I do, however, need to make sure you understand that your participation was not sanctioned by this office."

"Yeah...uh...obviously," Dan replied.

She nodded brusquely. "It is obvious, but I'm obligated to point it out. Now I would like to hear from you, in your own words, what happened. Please start from the beginning and leave out no details."

It took him almost an hour to describe his version of events. Agent Fox and Dragila occasionally asked clarifying questions. When he was done and they'd turned off the holorecorder, he asked, "Is Freya okay?"

"She's fine," Dragila said.

"Can I...contact her?"

"That's not up to us," Agent Fox said. "But I would like to discuss another issue with you."

"Okay," Dan said.

"Have you had a chance to think about whether you're going to keep your xenograft?" she asked.

"Uh...I hadn't thought about it. It's not hurting me, is it?"

"We've got investigators looking into Matrixeno and their bioengineers. Thus far, we have no reason to suspect the grafts are injurious," she said, "other than its effect on you in the presence of naked mole rats."

"So as long as I avoid Freya and don't visit the African savanna, I'm fine?"

Dragila smiled, but Agent Fox didn't seem to realize he was joking. "If you decide you'd like to have it removed or replaced with something more innocuous, the XIA can help with that. In fact, the issue I wanted to discuss concerns your graft. You're graduating high school in a few months. Have you ever considered working for law enforcement?"

Chapter Forty-four

The weekend, spent closeted in the XIA safe house with her mother, passed slowly for Freya.

The house was located about a quarter mile from Mouse's apartment and seemed like a castle in comparison to the places they'd lived recently. The XIA told them they could stay until her mother was able to secure work, which would allow them to move their things out of storage and into a new apartment.

They'd been debriefed, Freya had been officially interviewed, and the powers that be had assured them that Singh's death and the exposure of his crimes meant they were no longer in danger. Freya had her doubts, but she and her mother had discussed the future at length, and it was decided they would come out of hiding. Where they were going to live would depend on where her mom got work. In the meantime, Freya would continue to attend Temple Grandin High School, something she very much wanted to do.

She hadn't visited Dan or Mrs. Carson in the hospital; not because she was avoiding it, but because she had no way to get there. Her mother expressly forbade her from taking public transportation, a holdover from their days of hiding. When Freya pointed out that there were no longer any risks to being seen in public, her mother's face had frozen into a mask of uncertainty. It was a lot easier to talk about resuming their normal lives than it was putting it into action.

Monday morning, Freya arrived at school well before first bell. She hung out near the flagpole until her friends arrived. Kaye and Jin rushed over and hugged her as soon as they spotted her. Gev, Cindy, and Sandrew brought up the rear, all smiling – even Sandrew.

"Saw the news," he said. "Some crazy shit went down. Wasn't sure we'd see you today."

Freya knew from her interview that the XIA had spoken to each of them, as well as Gev's brother Cory.

"If it wasn't for you," she said, looking at each of their faces, "Dan wouldn't have found me. You guys are amazing."

"True." Sandrew performed a flourish with one hand and bowed.

"How is he?" Jin asked. "We heard he got hurt."

"I'm told he'll be fine." Freya looked around, hoping to see him. A few xenos had gathered atop the mound Kaye had referred to as the island of misfit boys, but no Dan or Bass. Wade, too, was noticeably absent.

"You haven't talked to him?" Gev asked.

"Not yet."

"So," Cindy said. "Is Freya even your real name?"

Freya laughed a little. "It's Amanda. Mandy."

Cindy made a face. "You want us to call you that? Because I like Freya better."

Gev looked like she was going to take Cindy to task, so Freya said quickly, "It's fine. To be honest, I kind of like it better than Mandy, too. I haven't been that girl in a long time."

"It'll be a nickname," Jin suggested, but Freya hardly heard. The hair on the back of her neck had lifted and chills radiated down her spine. She turned and there he was getting awkwardly out of a car. Bass was standing on the sidewalk holding a pair of crutches. Dan's sweatpants had been cut off at the thigh to accommodate the plaster cast that extended past his knee. When he'd settled his armpits onto the pads of the crutches, he lifted his gaze, spotted her, and smiled.

She made a beeline for him, and his smile spread into a wide grin. When she was close enough, he said, "You're here."

She shrugged a little, grinning shyly back. "Where else would I be?"

"I don't know. Resuming your old life?"

"Too boring," she declared.

Sandrew and the others gathered around Dan, offering congratulations and condolences.

"Surprised to see you here," Sandrew said. "I would have taken a week or two off to milk that leg for all it's worth."

"It's not that bad," Dan said. "Besides, I have some pretty compelling reasons to heal up fast."

"'Reasons'?" Cindy said, looking pointedly at Freya. "I think you mean 'reason.'"

"I think you're right," he replied.

Freya felt a blush heat her cheeks. She couldn't stop smiling. A fleeting wish for some alone time with Dan was quashed by the bell. Everyone accompanied him as he slowly made his way up the sidewalk.

He paused before entering the building. "Guys," he said.

"Yeah, yeah," Cindy interrupted. "We know. Freya already told us how awesome we are."

"You *are* awesome," Dan began.

"Don't sound so surprised," Sandrew said.

"Will you let the man talk?" Kaye exclaimed.

Dan laughed. "I just wanted to say thanks. Seriously. You have some mad skills."

"About those skills," Freya said.

Everyone looked at her.

"We could use your help finding a certain moppy little canine named Grover."

The end.

www.ingramcontent.com/pod-product-compliance
Lightning Source LLC
Chambersburg PA
CBHW061234170626
46809CB00007B/2673